LEVIAT

A Worldship Files book

By Erik Schubach

FIRST EDITION
ISBN 978-1687251022

CHAPTER 1
Irontown

I navigated my hovering Tac-Bike through the streets of Irontown on C-Ring, Beta-Stack. Another disturbance was reported in the bulkhead corridors. People moved out of the way as my warning beacon strobed. Air traffic was light and I considered heading above street level. This inner ring, like most of the inner rings, was inhabited mostly by Humans and a few unsavories like Sprites, witches, and a few shifters. Which is why I get dispatched here.

I usually get the shit calls, since I was Human too. Why should the Enforcers Brigade be any different than anyone else on the Worldship? Equal opportunity bigotry is the one thing leftover from the old world, that old home called Earth that is just a legend to most of us here on the Leviathan.

I've always thought the stories were just old folktales to keep us lower races in line, that idea that there ever was a place of Open Air, where machines and the ship's oxygen processing systems were not needed to keep us breathing, to keep us alive. But I have questioned it a few times when I've met a couple of the Old Earth Fae who say they were there on the day five thousand years ago when the Leviathan left the orbit of that dying planet.

And Fae... well everyone knows that the Fae cannot lie. Which makes them the best deceivers of all the races, they can spin the truth to make you believe anything they wish and not tell a single lie while doing it. And being in the Brigade, I've seen the outer rings, the lush forests and villages, and rivers that they modeled after Earth. I can almost imagine what it would be like if those forests went on forever instead of being constrained to just a mile wide strip in the fifty-mile diameter torus of the A-Rings.

It is hard to believe that each of the four A-Rings has almost two thousand square miles of space, four times that of the crowded C-Rings. Even more than the surface of the seven-mile diameter asteroid encased in the Heart sphere located... well located in the heart of the Leviathan. The workers and ore extractors there have virtually no gravity, so they can't even come farther out than the small D-Rings without requiring exoskeleton support or magic buffs to support their brittle bone structure in the higher gravity of the spinning rings.

I went past the outer markets then parked and mag-locked my Tactical Bike at one of the many entrances to the labyrinth of corridors, living, and working units of the slums in the bulkhead spaces, assigned to the people who couldn't afford to live outside in the cities and villages crowding the ring's environmental envelope.

An advertisement for cybernetic eye implants was playing across the door, damn taggers with their interactive graffiti were getting so commercial lately. Whatever happened to simple gang tagging or art expressionism? Now it was all about making an extra token chit or two.

I tapped a code on my wrist panel, to inform engineering to come out and strip the programmable paint from the structure as I just shook my head. It's no wonder us humans have such a bad reputation for being slacker trash that's only good for reclamation for fertilizer for the farms, or sucking hard vacuum in space.

It wasn't worth reviewing the surveillance footage to track down the tagger, it was a minor offense and wasn't worth having his or her meal cards set to rationing mode for a month. That sort of thing just promotes the rash of homeless in the lower rings when they can't eat properly to stay healthy enough to work. Not everyone had jobs that made enough chit to supplement their meal cards with fresh food if needed.

Sometimes as an Enforcer, we have to choose our battles. The others from Beta Squad, either call me soft because I let minor infractions like that slide, or null because, like all humans who weren't witches or shifters, had no magic of my own. Ahhh there's that Leviathan bigotry in action again.

Speaking of... a large tiger saw me step into the bulkhead corridors and it hissed and backed off as it changed to human and slipped into a living unit. Ok, maybe the Brigade isn't as popular here in the lower rings as elsewhere on the ship, or 'on the world' as we locals say.

I checked my wrist unit again, and muttered, "Oh go suck vacuum, Bulkhead J?" Of course, it would be the maintenance corridors out by the Skin. I sighed and started jogging through the semi-crowded corridors, people moving aside as I started the quarter-mile journey. I should have just taken my Tac-Bike like the entitled asses of the other squads do, siren wailing and forcing people out of the way.

The deeper I went, the fewer people I passed, until it was only the back hall vagrants. I kicked the hoof of a Satyr just to make sure he was still breathing. What the hells was he doing down here? When he groaned and opened his eyes, he started cursing me in Old Fairy. Who used Old Fairy anymore?

I snapped at him in the same tongue, "Get up, get out, and get sober."

He staggered to his hooves and took the bottle of spirits with him, muttering, "Fuckin' null." Ok, apparently he spoke Ship Common too.

I snorted and sighed, then started jogging toward the reported disturbance. Could they at least have classified it? Was it just someone shitting in the corridor or someone threatening to open a breach in the Skin?

On that thought, I paused at one of the massive breach seal blast doors as I passed from the section, at a sound. I saw flickering lights around the door seams of the emergency manual door release. I stepped over, shook my head then pulled the small door open and growled out, "Hey, get out of there, now! I'll pin your wings and haul your little asses in right now if you don't make yourselves scarce. And hey! Put that linkage back! We'd all be sucking vacuum if there was a meteoroid strike and this section decompressed without us being able to operate the door."

One of the glowing, five-inch tall humanoids with large moth-like wings hissed at me and waved me off. "Get lost, null."

I muttered to myself, "Sprites." Then I said as I pointed back toward the exit, "Out now, you filthy scavengers."

Two of the trio looked up from where they were trying to pull a linkage free, their eyes shooting from my face to my scatter armor to the badge and guns at my waist. They looked at their companion then took flight, leaving a trail of that damn itchy wing dust in their wake.

The third called after them in his... or her... or its squeaky voice; I always got pronoun headache with a three sex-species like Sprites, "Cowards! We can get ten chit for this!" Then it looked at me, harrumphed, then slammed the little access door in my face. The cheeky little shit.

I yanked it open again and the Sprite had the balls to cast at me. I didn't even bother dropping my talisman reinforced visor on my helmet with a thought. The spell sparked from its finger and dissipated against my scatter armor as it lived up to its namesake.

I reached into the box and grabbed the little ass by the wings, pinching them together as I hauled it out to hold up in front of my face. What had it been thinking, even without my armor, Sprites were the bottom of the magic community food chain, right below Faeries. The most it could accomplish against a human is to sting or make a slightly uncomfortable rash with its magic.

I asked as I cocked an eyebrow, "You want me to add assaulting an Enforcer to the list of charges? If you're lucky, they'll have you cleaning out grease traps in the food districts instead of the urinals in the D-Ring."

It swung little fists at my fingers uselessly as it dangled from its wings. "You're like all the other Bigs. If I were your size you'd be quaking in your fancy-schmancy boots like every other man."

"I'm a woman, are you visually impaired as well as stupid?"

It growled, "Man, woman? All you nulls look the same to me."

I sighed and said, "You aren't winning any points here." I scanned it with my wrist unit and an ID popped up. Ah, a third gender, a pollinator, I would have mistaken it for a girl, but I could see the feminine androgyny in it now. "Graz. No surname? You're not that old are you?"

The Fae and other preternatural races became known to the humans of Old Earth when they stepped forward to help construct the Leviathan so that all the races could escape the slowly expanding sun. In those days most preternatural people had only a single name. They didn't start taking surnames until a few hundred years after the Exodus launch to Eridani Prime, the new world our people will call home at the end of our ten thousand year journey.

We were only halfway there, and I and every Human on board would never see it, only the Fae and the Vampires had the chance of seeing the end of our voyage. Us Humans were not blessed with long lives, we burned bright for just around two centuries, then died. So it would still be thirty or forty generations before a human would set foot on the Ground, under Open Air.

It harrumphed and crossed its arms over its chest, and gods be damned if it wasn't cute as hell. "My parents were traditionalists, living on a farm, and couldn't pronounce grass right."

Answered like a true Fae, it wasn't exactly a yes or a no, why were they always so evasive? The lesser Fae could lie, unlike the Greater Fae.

I sighed and said, "I tell you what Graz, I'll overlook your little indiscretions if you just make yourself scarce and promise not to scavenge from critical emergency systems again. I'm on a disturbance call right now back at Bulkhead J, and don't have the time or desire to deal with you too, besides the paperwork is a bitch."

The purplish-pink color drained from Graz's face and it said, "Bulkhead J? The screaming? You don't want to go back there, it's..." The Sprite trailed off, shook its head and asked, "Just... it's better to walk away officer..."

I offered, "Shade, Knith Shade."

"Shade."

Letting the Sprite go, it buzzed its wings to stay in my face and asked, "You're going back there anyway, aren't you?" It actually looked scared... even though it was virtually immortal... well as long as nobody killed it.

I nodded. "It's my job."

The Sprite looked back the way I came as it licked its lips, contemplating my offer. Then it did the last thing I would expect a Sprite, which were flighty annoyances who looked out for only themselves, to do, and said, "I can show you where the screams came from."

Then it added quickly, "Not that I care what happens to another Big. Just if something happens to you, I'm stealing those MMGs you're carrying."

I snorted and patted my stunners, or Magic Mitigating Guns, as I pointed out, "Like you could even lift one, you flying rat."

It buzzed up and sat on my shoulder grabbing the edge of my helmet. "You've got a smart mouth for a Big." Then before I could retort Graz pointed, "That way." Then it muttered, "Shade means nobody." I knew that, but like everyone else, we don't pick our own names.

I sighed then started jogging in the direction it pointed. Gods... I hope nobody from the squad finds out I was taking directions from a Sprite.

CHAPTER 2
Organ Harvest

A few twists and turns later, always heading toward the outer Skin, we came upon a darkened corridor. I could see the emergency lighting had been not just disabled, but torn from their mounts in the ceiling.

Mother Fairy humper, that usually meant one thing. I didn't know there were any of 'them' in Beta, I thought they mostly stayed in the D-Rings of the Gamma and Delta Stacks. Away from the starshine that seems to pain them. I don't know how someone could choose a life in darkness for semi-immortality like that.

I've always had sharper night vision than most of the other Human Enforcers, and the lights from the various consoles and equipment indicators were enough for me to see by, but in this near-total darkness, things were still in dark shadow in places.

Then I almost jumped as I navigated around some of the huge life support pipes going down to the crossover levels under the surface of the ring, to a small, squeaky voice asking, "You can see down here?" I had almost forgotten Graz was with me, it had been pretty silent the moment we entered the back corridor next to the Skin.

I took a deep calming breath and whispered, "For the most part, there's still some pretty dark areas." Then I was blurting the curse I had just thought earlier, "Mother Fairy humper!" As the corridor brightened to daylight levels when the Sprite flared, dust sifting from its luminescent wings.

Blinking the spots out of my vision I growled, "Give a girl some warning first, Graz, you just about burned out my retinas."

I glanced at the living glow stick, to see the Sprite looking at me with suspicion. "I'm barely lit up, Shade."

Whatever. It was just that going from virtually no light to some light just seemed like the winged pain in the butt had sent up a flare in my vision. Graz supplied, "The screams came from the next cross corridor just there." After a hesitation, it asked, "You... you do know what lives back here don't you?"

I nodded. "I'm pretty sure I can guess, the disabled lighting is a dead giveaway."

Its wings buzzed in amusement as it giggled out, "Dead giveaway. Good pun, you're funny for a Big."

I rolled my eyes at its droll sense of humor and asked, "So, you're trinary, what pronouns am I supposed to be using? I can't keep thinking of you as it."

Graz blinked its oversize eyes that helped project that femininity to the otherwise androgynous mini thief. "It is fine, but I don't mind he or she either. We don't have the hangups you lesser races have with labels."

I snerked, "Lesser races? No labels just a little bigotry instead?"

"Hey! Did you call me little?" The Sprite flared purple and pink in warning, which decided things for me.

"Hey there, lady, don't get so defensive, I didn't call your tiny ass little."

"Go space yourself."

"You should be a little more grateful I'm not hauling your butt in right now."

"Well you should be grateful I'm showing you where the screams came from. And do you have some sort of fixation with my posterior or something? You humans are so strange."

I sighed, knowing it was idiotic to argue with a Sprite, but I'm a glutton for punishment it seems because I tapped my wrist console and it bloomed to life and I pointed at it. "I've got a map, genius."

She snorted then whispered, "It's right there."

I nodded and listened. My hearing was pretty good, but couldn't hear any movement or breathing around the corner. I pulled a MMG in one hand and a telescoping cold iron baton in the other and snicked it out as quietly as I could with a flick of my wrist. Graz hissed and shied away from the cold iron as I said, "Stay behind me, the last thing I need is for a civilian to get hurt while I'm on a call."

The diminutive person extinguished the glow from her wings and body and buzzed up into the pipes and conduits in the overhead space. I stopped breathing to listen again, I could just make out a lapping sound. I stepped around the corner calling out, "Enforcer!"

The sight in front of me on the deck plates had me diving to my knees to place two of my gloved fingers on the unmoving person, who was bleeding out onto the deck from a clean but deep looking cut in his bare abdomen. My glove feedback didn't detect a heartbeat as I tried to determine the race of the victim.

I scanned them with my wrist console and furrowed my brow in confusion, what was a Woodling? I know there were countless races of preternatural onboard, and I have only met a few dozen at most since I rarely ventured into the A or B-Rings where the older species and Fae lived. I noted the dust on the floor by his head and the stumps sticking out of his coarse brown fur.

Someone had sawed off his horns or antlers, and the incision in his abdomen looked too clean like possibly a laser scalpel had done it. I felt the blood drain from my face. I knew what this was... I got on my coms and said, "Control, this is Shade, badge alpha three four eight niner. We need crime techs at my location. There's been an unauthorized organ harvest here. Victim is deceased." I looked at my console and read off the man's identity. "Mother has identified the victim as Reiner Katan, approximate time of death..." I scrolled the info from my scan, "Sixteen twenty-three ship time."

Mother was the name of the Leviathan's AI Computer Core, I'm sure it was an acronym back in the early years but to heck, I doubt if anyone knows what it stands for now without having to do a database lookup. Everyone on the world just calls her Mother.

Control confirmed and I prompted as my brows furrowed when I couldn't pull up surveillance for this section, "I need access to the video feeds, my location for the past thirty minutes, Mother isn't supplying them."

Control responded with, "The video feeds went down in that area over an hour ago, they've just went live again forty-five seconds ago. Probably Sprites, the vermin have been mucking up systems in the C-Rings lately." Then the woman said, "Mab preserve us, the poor bastard." She must have just seen the victim beside me.

I looked up to a glowing red light that hadn't been there earlier and shrugged apologetically at the camera, then severed the link so I could get back to work and examine the scene. It was going to be a bitch if the cameras were down since that meant even biometrics and magic imprint scans wouldn't be available either. I noted Graz was still bristling at the vermin comment from Control, as she hovered obstinately with her arms crossed over her chest in the ceiling space.

I heard a slurping behind me and spun, a gods be damned Vampire had move in and was crouched right behind me, licking up the blood on the deck. It started to blur away when it saw my attention on it, but I slashed out with the baton and stopped it as I blurted, "Stop right there! Consider yourself bound by law. This is a crime scene."

It hissed and leaped, trying to blur again, but I was able to catch his foot and yanked him back to the deck. I dropped my MMG, it would be next to useless against a vamp, even at a high charge. It tried to push me back with its superior strength, but I caught his wrists and bent them back hard enough I could feel the bones grinding on each other.

Then it was in my face, hissing, its pupils dilating, I didn't bother signaling my visor to drop to block him out, and his black eyes threatened to swallow my world. I shook off its attempt to glamour me. Damn Vampires. Luckily, in training, I was one of the few who had a strong enough will that I could blunt the effects of their mental whammy. I saw some of the biggest men, even a centaur be reduced to a groveling lovestruck fool by Gemma, the only Vampire in the Brigade, who taught Defense Against Vampires at the academy.

She had been everything you hear about vampires, with flawless beauty, grace, and unfortunately, no heartbeat. The whole being dead thing turned me off or she would have been in some of my more interesting fantasies.

But this guy? I head-butted him, shattering his nose with my helmet, and used the few moments of distraction the healing of the damage would take him to slap a mag-band on his wrist. He looked from my eyes, his rage turning to surprise when he looked down as I smirked and whispered, "Lockdown," to my wrist console, and the mag-band activated, pulling his arm roughly to the deck with the equivalent of ten Gs of gravity.

He screeched, and I noted he was nothing like Gemma, if he cleaned himself up, he'd probably be a beautiful man, but covered in grime and blood, his hair a ratted mess, he looked more like the corpse he was than a pretty lure for weak-minded people. Their beauty and grace was how they used to hunt, before the Leviathan.

He calmed a little and pleaded, "I didn't do this. I'm just so hungry, all that blood getting cold."

I looked at him and shook my head. "I know you didn't, but you know as well as I do that consuming any blood outside your daily rations from Med-Tech is illegal. And you're a witness to this."

He started to lunge as close as he could with his arm pinned to the deck plate but he screeched and recoiled, pulling himself into a fetal position when light flared around us as bright as a million stars. Well fine, it just seemed like it was that bright in the near-total darkness around us. I blinked away the spots again to see Graz in front of the cowering Vampire, she was holding a little piece of metal fashioned into a blade as she said, "I'm in the ultraviolet spectrum right now you animated corpse." Then she looked at me, with a self-satisfied smirk. "He was trying to get to your wrist control."

I nodded. "I got that, Graz. I have this handled..." I trailed off at something glinting between two conduits on the deck. I didn't see it until the Sprite flared. I took out an evidence bag from my belt and scooped it up. It looked to be some sort of archaic, non-powered surgical implement from a museum or something.

The Vampire was whimpering and I saw his skin bubbling. Huh, who knew a Sprite could glow in the ultraviolet and could bring down one of the deadliest predators on the world like this. I said, "That's enough, Graz, I need him alive... well alive-ish. We can't have him igniting."

The mini person huffed. "Fine." Then went dark and all the shadows returned.

I looked at the Vampire as his skin healed and asked, "What did you see?"

He shook his head as he sat up and tried to tug his arm free from the floor. "Nothing, I heard the screaming and called in the disturbance, these are my halls, where I nest. But then I smelled the blood. By the time I arrived here there wasn't anyone here but the body and the blood... and you ruined my feeding."

He was the one who called it in? A vamp as a good samaritan, now I've seen everything. I tended to believe him, and I really didn't want to have to muzzle him so he wouldn't bite me when I took him to processing on my Tac-Bike for his unauthorized feeding.

I sighed and said, "If I tag you, so I can do any followup questioning later that I may need, then you're free to go."

He was just nodding in earnest and I sighed then tapped the code on my console and I heard the radioactive dye inject into his arm that would light up like a beacon on the Leviathan's internal scanners. Then I released the strap and he sat back and rubbed his wrist as I told him, "Now make yourself scarce, the crime techs and coroner will be here any moment. And if I ever hear of you drinking anything other than your daily stipend of blood, I'll rain down upon you like hellfire, do we understand each other?"

He nodded and said, "Yes, Enforcer..." He left an open question as I scanned him for identity and race, though race was imminently apparent.

I supplied, "Shade."

He inclined his head and then blurred. This time I let him go. I checked the tracking on my wrist console, looked at the surgical implement in the bag, then the corpse and said, "All I wanted was just one quiet day, but instead I find the fifth organ harvest on the world in the past month."

"Sucks to be you."

I chuckled and agreed with her assessment, "Yes. Yes, it does, Graz. And for a micro pain, you're ok. Your good-intentioned assist is appreciated." Making sure not to make the mistake of thanking her.

She shrugged. "I was bored, you ruined my fun back there, so I thought what the heck."

CHAPTER 3
Remnants

By the time the techs were done processing the scene, all I wanted was to get to my quarters and sleep for a week.

I had spent an hour on coms and holo with Control as we tried to coax some sensor or video from the surrounding area to see if we could get a clue as to how our deceased wound up back here and without his horns and whatever was surgically removed from him. We'd have to wait for the coroner's report in the morning to know just what was taken. They'd have to do a Magic Resonance Scan to map every molecule of the decedent's remains to store on Mother. What can't we do today with modern magi-tech?

A disturbing fact was that the area was devoid of any DNA trace evidence, only the murdered Woodling's DNA was found. Every living thing is constantly shedding DNA when we breathe, when we shed skin cells, and there is transfer whenever we touch something, like the surgical implement I had in the evidence bag, which the techs scanned through the smart-plastic to find no DNA or prints either.

That in itself wouldn't be so alarming, but when I say they found no trace DNA in the area, I mean, none at all, not mine, not Graz's, not the vampire's... what was his name?

I was too exhausted to check my wrist control so blinked twice to activate the heads up display in my helmet and the data was projected directly into my retina. I winced. I didn't like using it because as I said, I have great night vision so the display was annoyingly bright.

Ah, here it is... I flicked my finger though the log my armor kept for me automatically, Thase Tanda. I switched to visual logs to see my interaction with him. I caught movement behind him, over his shoulder farther back in the corridor. I narrowed my eyes, and said, "Stop. Go back to index 541.2 freeze. Isolate cross corridor..." I looked at the bulkhead marking and continued, "J-51 and access-way 399. Zoom and enhance."

I stared at the display hovering in front of my eyes, there was a shadow half over a life support display panel. Someone was there. "Mother? Can you cycle through light spectrums from this visual scan and interpolate into the visible spectrum?" I almost jumped at the soft throaty alto of Mother's voice. I forgot that since I was using my suit's systems audio would be active too. Her voice always made me a bit nervous, unlike other Artificial Intelligences, she didn't have any of the little telltale indications that she was just a computer, she always sounded far too real to me and I swear her emotions couldn't be just simulations.

Ok, so she creeped me the fuck out, but despite myself, I really liked her.

She virtually purred at me. "There you are Knith, you've been ignoring me ever since you arrived on scene. I'd be happy to assist." At one second intervals, the view changed, ultraviolet and infrared had more detail than the visible spectrum, almost as if it were being blocked somehow. I wouldn't ever have noticed except it had moved, blocking part of the display down the corridor.

I stopped once Mother went into the extreme infrared range, over one thousand nanometers and said, "There! Can you overlay and clean it up a bit?"

Her reply was almost chirpy. "You bet. Here you go."

When the false color image was overlapped on the shadow I could make out... "Is that a hand?" She sharpened it a bit, and I squinted like it would make me see the light blob any better. But I was sure, there was a pale hand with something that looked like a silver ring shaped like some sort of talon, on the thumb.

I exhaled, and said, "Save that to the case file please." Then I asked, already knowing the answer, "Mother, how many races wear silver rings on their thumbs?"

She chuckled at me. "Anyone can wear a ring on their thumb, Knith."

I sighed, and said, "I know, please humor me, you're seeing what I am... best guess."

"My best guess isn't admissible as evidence in a..."

"I know, Mother, I'm just wanting you to tell me what I already know."

She sighed, the computer actually sighed at me, and she supplied, "It appears to be a Fae silver Ionga ring. And again, that doesn't mean anything as anyone, even you could wear one."

I growled out, "What are the odds?"

She purred, "No need to get grumpy. There is a five-point seven percent probability that someone outside of the two courts of greater Fae is wearing it."

My heart stopped for a moment. Well fuck me sideways and space me naked. Did a greater Fae witness the harvesting and subsequent murder? Were they... I hated where my head was going... were they involved somehow?

Shit shit shit... I didn't voice that. Just doing that would have Control coming down on me like a metric ton of Fairy droppings. Even intimating that a greater Fae could be involved would get me busted back to mining security and the Fae could punish the whole ring for the insult.

Instead, I asked, "Possible reasons for the area be free of any trace DNA?"

She seemed as eager as me to change topics. "I take it you didn't sterilize the area yourself?"

I sighed. "You have access to my sensors and logs on the case, you tell me..." I paused, I had almost called her a smartass. Just a computer, Knith.

Ok, she chuckled again and said, "There is a ninety-seven point one percent probability that a sanctum spell has been cast on the area."

With a thought, my visor slipped down, sealing airtight, and the hiss of my re-breather venting my CO_2 as I exhaled was loud in my ears until the sound canceling magi-tech kicked in. I touched a talisman I had in one of my belt pouches and looked around.

I could see the spelled gear, and some of the magi-tech the crime scene techs had as they packed up. Then took in the area as a whole and could see two concentric circles extending through the physical walls with some of the most complex sigils pulsing and spinning as the two fading circles rotated in opposite directions, then I looked up to see two matching circles going vertical creating a sphere of magical influence, I didn't know diddly squat about magic, but I knew the difference between Fae and witch magic.

Any human... any person, could use magic, just like I was doing now, but we required talismans or some other physical tool like potions or a focus to activate whatever spell is imbued in the tool. The only humans who could cast spells were witches, and their magic was inelegant, brute force botches that ate away at their bodies, compared to the finely spun silver artwork of Fae spells.

Mab preserve us all, a Fae sanctum spell, and a pale hand with an Ionga, or talon ring. I didn't like where this was going. Instead of voicing my growing suspicion, I asked in a hoarse voice, "Logged?"

Mother said, "Of course, Knith. You aren't thinking that..."

I cut her off as my visor flipped up into my helmet. "Circumstantial. Can you feed me the case files of the other Harvestings? I want to go over the crime scenes and the coroner reports. Even the gods be damned MRSs."

She seemed glad I was looking at other possibilities, just as I was. "Already downloaded into your suit."

"Thanks, Mother. Hey, do you happen to know who on the world I can speak with about ancient medical equipment like this one?" I indicated the evidence bag.

She said, "Hmm... besides the historian at the medical sciences library in the Alpha-Stack, B-Ring, there is nobody 'on the world' who has the expertise."

Ok, why did she stress the three words, on the world? Then my heart sank as I muttered like my life was over, "Remnants."

"That's why I like you so much Knith, always so positive and upbeat."

"Sarcasm? Really? Does that compute?"

She seemed put out as she harrumphed. Ok, maybe I was being harsh, "I'm sorry Mother, I just hate dealing with those who chose to live off the world. I always feel like I have to check to make sure I still have all my gear after I leave a Remnant. And half of them are on the trunk, not stealing free gravity from the rings."

If she were a real person, I swear she'd be smiling as she chirped out, "Well good news, this one is mag locked to an airlock down on D-Ring of the Beta-Stack."

An icon bloomed on a schematic of the Leviathan. Fifteen miles inside the ring to a spoke, and then six miles back on the D-Ring not bad. But most people would be heading home or to assigned quarters, so it would take the better part of an hour to navigate the crowds on my Tac-Bike. Or I could... "How far to the closest Jumper?"

The ring bloomed with twenty icons, one just a mile away. I'd have to lock down my bike here, but the Jump Pods would get me to the D-Ring in a minute or two. I'd have to take a public tram back to the airlock location, but I didn't want to be in that area of the D-Ring when the Day Lights went out.

I said, "Thanks, Mother, then blinked twice to shut down the heads up and silence her. "You are welcome Knith. I'm here if you need me."

As I jogged back out toward my bike, I passed the crime techs loading up a mag-sled, I handed the evidence bag to a young elf woman, who pressed her thumb on my wrist console to transfer the chain of evidence.

Then when everyone was out of view a blur of light swooped down from the overhead, to land on my shoulder. A squeaky voice asking, "What we doing now, Shade?"

I looked at the Sprite. "I'm investigating, you're doing whatever it is you do. This isn't any of your concern. If I need anything else from you, I'll find you."

Graz shrugged and said, "Whatever," but made no move to leave. What was her problem?

I ignored her and tapped in my location on the navigation console and let my bike do the driving as I started reviewing the nearby video and scan data around the time of the murder on my heads up.

"So where did you say we were going?"

My left eye twitched, and I made a point of ignoring the winged nuisance, and then paused the playback when I saw the victim heading through the market, his long curled horns making it easy to track him. He hesitated and looked between some booths and pointed at himself, a questioning look on his shaggy face.

Then he went between them and I lost track of him as I sifted through differing angles and noted the scan data was reporting nothing in that area... not that it was empty, it was that there was no data, like it was being blocked. Magic again?

"World to Shade."

I exhaled, realizing my master plan of ignoring Graz until she went away wasn't going to work. I looked at her and said, "Going to visit a Remnant."

"Ooooo which one?"

I looked at the info Mother provided. "Mac... one name, no race, no other data... he's not in the system other than the designation as a peddler of antiquities and... information. And his hull number."

Graz whistled. "That old null coot? He's stingy with the chit tokens when I bring him grade A..." She trailed off.

I cocked an eyebrow and smirked and finished, "Contraband?"

Ok, I had to chuckle at the look of shock and indignation the Sprite gave me as she blinked her oversize eyes innocently, "Contraband? Me?" Against my better judgment, I liked this small person.

I told her, "Now shush, I'm going over some data."

She nodded and mimed zipping her lips and then hesitated and made an unzipping motion. "You sure you're just a null and not a shifter?"

"Why would you ask that?"

"I've just never seen a human move as fast as you, or see in the dark like you. You stopped a Vampire from blurring, you moved so fast. And when he tried to glamour you, you just shook it off."

I sighed. "I've trained and sparred with all sorts of races for over twenty-five years in the Brigade. I've just honed my reflexes by necessity to stop from getting my head torn off in sparring matches with shifters, Elves, and Minotaurs. And I've just got a strong will. That's what the Defense Against Vampires instructor at the academy told me."

Before she could inundate me with a million more questions, I mimed zipping her lips and went back to my investigation.

I sighed as we pulled up at the Jump terminal. I really hated going to the Remnants... the positively ancient and archaic flying wrecks that had been part of the construction force which built the Leviathan over a thousand years. When the names of the captains of those vessels weren't called in the worldwide lottery to be one of the lucky twelve million people to populate the Worldship, they attached their vessels to the hull of the ship.

They survive by trading services, old tech, or sex to the people on the world for chit tokens or food cards. As they are not technically living on the world, or considered part of her compliment, they are treated as foreigners, their ships outside the purview of our laws. They are tolerated by the powers that be as long as they agree to abide by the laws of the world when they step out of their vessels.

One rumor is that some of the Remnants are still kept space-worthy by their owners. And another rumor is that minor witches, clairvoyants, and fortune tellers are said to be on the old floating relics. Many people discount that and write it off to the people living on the ancient ships swindling naive people out of chits.

I locked my bike down outside the terminal, there was always one of the dozen or so Jumper tubes available at the terminals as they weren't the most desirable way to travel between rings, but they were so much faster. As expected, there was no line, so I swallowed as I stepped into the clear tube with the compressed gas thrusters at the top and bottom of it. I really hated free-floating in space in these glorified coffins, with nothing but translucent plastic, spelled against micrometeoroids, between myself and hard vacuum.

I looked at Graz. "You sure you want to do this?"

Without waiting for an answer I hit the D-Ring designator and the floor opened up under us. The lower decks shot past, then with a thwump we were shooting through space ballistically down to the receiver port on the D-Ring below us.

A squeaky voice next to my ear giggled and asked, "Are you

seriously closing your eyes? For a Big, you're awfully queasy about things."

I had to open my eyes when she trailed off with an awestruck, "Ooooooooh."

Then I smiled in wonder as the majesty of the nebula we were flying past at fractional C speed took up my entire view, punctuated by an endless starfield so bright I had to shade my eyes from the bright points of light. There had to be gods, to have created something so beautiful in the universe. I felt so very... small.

"Wow."

CHAPTER 4
Dirty Deeds Done Dirt Cheap

When we stepped out onto the deck of the D-Ring, I had to catch myself, there was only point three of a G here and I bounded off the deck a couple inches when I went to stride normally.

In the Brigade we trained almost daily in both Zero-G and in one point two five G so that we weren't slowed down in any environment on the world in executing our duties as Enforcers. I got my sea legs after a few steps and headed for a mag-tram.

I looked around the area as I stepped out into the open ring area, the air was heavy with a fog that the atmospheric processors couldn't keep up with, from the smelting plants and ore refinement and resource extraction that occurred in this sector.

This made me look absently out the horizon of the ring to the trunk of the Leviathan where the spherical structure enclosing the seven-mile wide asteroid at the core of the ship has been mined daily over the past five thousand years. They say all the resources would be exhausted in the next couple thousand years. The output of many metals, gasses, and water is just twenty percent of the levels back in the first days after Exodus.

The D-Rings were almost purely industrial with virtually no green spaces, and the canal around the center of the ring was an algae bath that provided much of the oxygen for the level. It smelled like the small swamp and bog areas in sections of the B-

Rings, and the smell mingled with the smoke from the smelting and extraction plants to produce a uniquely sour odor. The bulk of the food production down here had to be done in enclosed domes.

I know many people are assigned duties here, or their families have been here for countless generations and it was all that they knew. It was the people who chose to be here that I didn't understand, but we all have our reasons for the choices we make. I chose to join the Brigade after I went through the university in my Ring. Being a Clinic Child, or CC, I had no family and was raised by the Reproduction Clinic. My genes were selected by some lab tech and I was grown in an artificial womb with the other embryos to keep static Equilibrium of the human population.

Whenever any race's birth rates were down, the clinics, well, the clinics grew more to keep the world's population at twelve million. So I was born forty-six years ago in the clinic, and the lesser Fae nurses were responsible for giving us 'designations', our names. They were obviously bored or were of the same opinion that we nulls aren't worth their time as they gave me the Shade surname... meaning 'nobody'... since that was what we Clinic Children were, especially us Humans, nobodies. No family, no home, nothing.

Through my entire childhood I grew up with that knowledge, and told how I only existed to keep a population quota and nothing I did would ever amount to anything. I pushed back and excelled in school, then the university, and then I joined the Brigade to protect people and make a difference, thumbing my nose at those who thought I was just shade.

Graz saw me staring off across the industrial complex and made an unzipping motion in front of her lips and said, "You've been an Enforcer for twenty-five years? I know all you Big nulls look the same to me, and you only live as long as a sneeze, but even I know you are still just a fledgling."

I squinted at her on my shoulder and made a show of re-zipping her lips. "I've always looked young for my age. I may look to be just barely an adult, but I'm a quarter way through my life. It is the bane of my existence, as nobody at Control takes me very seriously, and is why I still ride a beat on a C-Ring."

I huffed and started to push through the crowds of people heading home to their quarters. "I don't even know why I'm telling you this. My story isn't any different than anyone else on the world."

Then I moved over to help a Faun who had stumbled and dropped the packages she was carrying. "Here, let me help, miss."

She looked up at me, her big doe eyes blinking, and she smiled. It looked damn cute on her tawny furred face. I handed her the packages and she said in the soft tones her race was known for, "Thank you, Enforcer."

Smiling, I assured her, "No problem at all, have a good night." She scurried off in leaping bounds, completely at home in the low gravity here. I took a moment to admire her feminine form.

I glanced over to see Graz studying me carefully like she was trying to figure me out as I grumped out, "What?"

She pointed at her lips, keeping them shut, and shrugged. Smartass.

We hopped a crowded mag-tram and I felt a little uncomfortable as everyone gave me a wide berth. And before long we stepped off onto a street closest to the airlock. We headed to the bulkhead and into the winding corridors back to this ring's Bulkhead J and the Skin.

Unlike where poor Mr. Katan was killed, the lights were all operational here, and there were still a lot of people milling about the corridors near the wide red and white warning stripes around the airlock door.

I blinked twice and sighed at the necessity. "Mother?"

She purred out, "Here Knith."

"I want to live log this instead of using my suit's systems outside the Skin."

"Understood. Hey, buck up, it'll be ok."

I snorted. "Ok, I have to admit, you're funny at times."

She sounded pleased as she chirped out, "Thank you."

Then we stepped through the inner door, which should have been closed. I looked over to see someone had opened the manual control overrides and a bar of metal was holding the release lever down. I sighed and yanked the bar out and threw it on the deck-plates as the inner door closed behind me. I was muttering, "There's a reason its called an airlock and not a hallway." Ok, was that Graz or Mother who snickered at my bad mood?

At least they hadn't jury-rigged the outer door, not that they could since there was no manual release for it by necessity. By habit, I checked the series of green hard seal indicators showing that pressure was equalized between the world and the Remnant beyond.

I looked at the overlay Mother automatically displayed in my peripheral, anticipating my need, and I saw this was a small cluster of remnants that were docked with the larger vessel sealed to the outer skin of the world, airlock to airlock.

Once I hit the control, the huge bolts retracted and the gears turned, releasing the door seals as it slid up into its frame. And I glanced inside the positively archaic corridor beyond, its inner airlock door held open like the one on the world had been, as people hustled about. Something was playing over the ship's intercom. Music I wasn't familiar with. It had a hard edge to it like the stuff they played at the taverns in the Human districts.

I caught the beat and found that whatever it was, had a good hook to it, even though the vocals were in some form of archaic English, which was the root language of Ship Common. "Mother, what is that?" I pointed to the air. I listened to the words, glad now that Old English was a requirement at the university.

She said flatly, "Music."

"I know that. I mean what is it? I'm not familiar with this style. I like it."

She responded like I was off my rocker for liking it, "It is from the anthropological records of Old Earth, from the twentieth century, some of the first magnetic media archives later converted to digital. The style is called rock, and the title is "Dirty Deeds Done Dirt Cheap"."

I smirked at that as I looked farther into what could only be described as a den for the unsavory characters of the world. "Apropos. Considering." The title words sang out with the hook I found I liked. Was this really from the twentieth century? That was what, eight or nine hundred thousand years ago, and it still made me tap my fingers on my leg to the beat? I guess music is one of those timeless mediums, and the words spoke to me.

With a couple of motions of my fingers in the virtual display, I moved this section of the anthropological music section to my personal playlist. It reminded me of the rebellious Irontown Clank music I grew up with.

I found myself smiling as I made my way down the corridor. Past an obviously drunk or chemically impaired couple of humans, the men were in a sloppy lip-lock until they saw my uniform and scurried into a cabin with strings of beads obscuring the doorway.

We were on the right deck, and by the bulkhead markings, I was just a few cabins away from the owner of this ancient wreck. I hesitated at one door that had a sign for an oracle. What were the odds Madame Zoe was a charlatan? Clairvoyance was a really rare form of witchery.

When an older woman, possibly a hundred eighty or ninety with honest to goodness spectacles slid the mechanical door open to look at me expectantly, I swallowed and moved quickly down the corridor. Had she known I had hesitated by her door? I looked back to see her just watching me.

Charlatan or not, clairvoyants unnerved me.

Then I took a second to square my eyes on an impromptu map of the Remnant cluster painted on the wall with interactive paint so that I'd have a record of it I could look at later. I almost snorted as I started to move and the red X that said 'you are here' changed to 'now you are here' as I moved and the X moved. Clever.

I rolled my eyes at the flashing lights by the lift at the end of the corridor, with a big blinking arrow pointing down with 'Brothel' glowing in nice big letters. This really was where the dregs of society made a home, wasn't it? But a part of me kind of liked it in a rebellious sort of way. They knew who they were and weren't ashamed to show it.

Ah, here we were A1, captain's quarters. Graz was pointing at the door just in case I was some sort of incompetent nitwit or something. I gave her a warning glare and she ignored me, just sifting her dust to my shoulder as she kicked her feet nonchalantly.

I looked around and then banged on the metal door, noting Graz was sort of shying away from the unpainted surface as she held on tightly to my helmet. My eyes widened, was the ship's bulkheads made of iron or steel?

A moment later the door slid up to reveal a stocky middle-aged

man of maybe a hundred, with a rugged look and salt and pepper
beard that matched his shoulder-length hair. I noted he wore a
severely outdated exoskeleton, telling me he likely left the D-Ring
where he was stealing free rotation for gravity to deal in the upper
Rings of the Stacks.

That or as a deterrent against any unsavory who thought they
could make off with all the wondrous stuff I could see covering the
walls behind him. Trinkets and gadgets and things that looked so
antique I wouldn't even be able to guess as to what they might be.

His gruff voice was exactly what I had expected as he asked in
false courtesy while keeping his arm barred across the gap of the
doorway. "Ah, Enforcer. What brings you to the Underhill today?"

I felt the corner of my lips twitch involuntarily, trying to smile at
the ship's name. Underhill was the legendary home of the Fairy
folk, the Fae, where they hid from the humans back on Earth before
they revealed themselves to offer aid in constructing the Worldship.
And in exchange for solving some of the problems that the humans
still didn't have a solution for, they bartered guaranteed free passage
with the Exodus launch.

Again I thought it was apropos.

I thought of how things must have been when all the races had
agreed to a lottery, and how the Fae were tricky in their negotiations.
Humans thought they were being the tricky ones when the Fae had
agreed for the other races to just two million souls and giving ten
million seats to the humans who numbered almost thirty billion on

Old Earth at the time.

The humans thought the other races would have similar lotteries to see which people would leave Earth on the Leviathan, leaving the rest behind. But it was us Humans who learned that every Fae had an angle, they never spoke plainly, and used truth as a weapon to deceive. All of the other races of preternatural, including all of the Fae, had just shy of the two million souls, so the entirety of all their races were saved.

Then the Fae Unseelie Winter Queen, Mab, sold the remaining seats to the richest or most politically powerful of the human families who didn't win in the lotteries. And not for money, but for their power and influence in the shape of favors. Favors those influential families were still paying off all these generations later here on the world. Never ever ever put yourself in a position of owing a Fae a favor, and never ever ever thank them, as they will see it as you admitting to being in their debt.

I asked, "Mac?"

He nodded and pointed out, "You are aware that you aren't on the world now, Enforcer? Your jurisdiction ended back at the Skin there." He nudged his chin down the corridor to the airlock.

I had to smile at the sly man and said, "Enforcer Knith Shade, and I'm not here for you, just some information."

He looked at my shoulder and prompted, "This one your prisoner?"

Graz mimed unzipping her lips and squeaked out, "You wish,

you old space fart. I'm helping the Big here."

"You owe me three transducers for the bum lot you pawned off on me last time, you winged rat."

"Buyer beware. You paid me under market value that last four times, so you got what I gave."

I cleared my throat and they stopped discussing things I'm sure I shouldn't be privy to. The man looked me up and down and said flatly, "Information isn't free."

I sighed and pulled this month's meal card out of a pouch on my belt. I lived at and ate at the Brigade barracks so I never used my ration card. "It's full."

He snatched it out of my fingers like he thought I'd change my mind, and as he pocketed it he moved aside, ushering me into his eclectic wonderland of amazing items. "By all means, Knith, come on in. You're not an Enforcer here in Underhill. And I'm not calling you Shade, it means..." I held a hand up nodding as I moved past. I was well aware of what it meant.

I moved up to one of the bulkheads to look at the hundreds of items hanging from hooks as Graz flew down to perch on the back of what looked to be a comfortable, overstuffed leather chair. Taking only one down-stroke of her moth-like wings to make the journey in the low gravity, like she had done it a thousand times. Hell, maybe she had. She probably dealt with Mac's father and countless generations before him.

I was lifting what looked to be some sort of circuit tester with ports all along the front while Mac was studying my face as he said, "You break it you bought it." Then he took it from my hands and brought it to his mouth and blew into it and it made music, as he cupped it in his hands to make few notes as he slid his mouth along it. "It's called a harmon-ka. From Old Earth. Very rare. You like?"

Mother was correcting him in my ear. "The proper name is harmonica. It is similar to the modern photonic slide flutes of..." I huffed and she stopped.

He caught my interaction then pointed at my eyes where he probably saw the heads up flickering in my retinas. "Off."

I nodded and said sweetly to the air, "Goodbye, Mother."

"Knith, don't you dare shut off the feed. This..."

I tapped the privacy mode icon on the virtual control pad in front of my eyes and my entire scanning and observation system powered down, and my connection to Control and Mother shifted to standby. She was going to give me a good what for when I activated the feed again, she hated being ignored, and that made some part of me smile. She never got upset when Kahn or the others put her in visual mode only. I actually liked talking to her, when she wasn't being so bossy and overbearing like this.

I growled when he was about to start talking, and said as I watched the system's ready lights start to flicker, "Just a second. Mother is hacking me." I physically powered down my armored uniform and smirked at it as I said to the air, "Hack that you, you mothering AI. I can handle myself."

This got the man to snort and clap a hand on my shoulder. "Ok, you... I like. So have a seat and tell me what kind of information you're looking for."

He set the harmonica down on a table filled with relics from another time beside the other chair he sat in. I said, "I'm currently investigating a series of murders on the world, illegal organ harvesting, and..."

He held a hand up, looking almost angry. "That isn't the sort of thing we deal in down here. You can go space yourself if you..."

I stopped him with a look. "We don't think you had anything to do with it. I just found an item at the last crime scene that looks like some sort of antique surgical implement that we hoped you might be able to identify and possibly point me at anyone on the world who might still use that sort of thing."

He relaxed then said, "Well let's have a look then."

I blinked at him then snorted and said, "Mab preserve us all. Just a second, I have the scans on my suit's storage. Mother is going to kill me."

The man chuckled. "That's what happens when you become too dependent on magic or technology. Power her up."

The suit powered back up and Mother's voice filled my ears, she was still off on a rant, hadn't her subroutines shown I had logged out?

I tried to get a word in, and it took Mac leaning in toward me and saying, "Hello, Mother," to get her to stop.

She hacked my public address speaker and started saying clinically and robotically, "Mac, master of the Underhill, hull number AJAX-43. Suspected in multiple stolen property complaints, no outstanding warrants. Three stints in ore extraction for various charges ranging from..."

He said, "Good to hear your voice again too, you overrated tin can."

I stepped in before their verbal sparring went on into the night. "Mother, please. Let me do my job."

Did she harrumph? And why did Mac look so self-satisfied as he sat back in his chair, arms crossed behind his head? He had tried to get a rise out of her, hadn't he?

I tapped on my wrist console and pulled up the scans of the implement. I looked around and saw holo-projectors at the ceiling so I accessed them and the item materialized in the air in front of him. He reached up and my eyes widened when he took it between his fingers to examine it.

He had coherent photon projectors in this floating junk heap? That was A or B-Ring tech for the rich. He looped a finger and all my scan data appeared beside his hand, scrolling along as he nodded appreciatively.

With surety, he said, "It's a manual scalpel. This is real old school. No photonic laser blades. No incision-less sonic subdural features. Some of the old back alley clinics still use these types of tools."

I opened my mouth to ask for a list but he was already shaking his head at me. "But you won't find the owner of it down here, or in any of the lower rings."

Before I could ask why, he pointed at the data stream and said, "See here, this is silver, not stainless steel. This is Fae."

Ok, that was a leap, yes the Fae wouldn't be able to touch stainless steel without gloves or they would burn their fingers, but just because it was silver didn't mean...

He made a stretching motion with two fingers and the projection grew multiple times its actual size and he pointed at a fine carving at the base of the handle. It was an intricate spellwork circle with finely etched runes around it and a symbol in the middle I recognized from somewhere. It was such fine craftsmanship and micro-etched with magic, as the measurements of the circle were displayed, I realized it would look like a simple dot to the naked eye.

I sighed, he was right, it was Fae in origin, and I bet if I looked up the spells, they would give the implement the same properties as our modern laser scalpels. This was three pieces of evidence pointing the one place I dared not follow. I pointed. "That symbol looks familiar."

He nodded and shut down the projection. "It should, it is a family crest." He shook his head when he saw the question forming on my lips and Mac said as he stood, "I'm sorry Knith, that's all I can say. I probably just put a target on myself. I suggest you don't dig any farther."

He hesitated and looked at me, then the table and he handed me the harmonica. "A month's rations is too much for the trouble I just heaped on you. Heed my advice? Let this drop." The man was nervous about something.

He stood at the door and put on a smile as I looked at the harmonica, then slipped it into a pouch and moved to the door as Graz landed on my shoulder, uncharacteristically silent. Mac said, "You never know when a little music might save your life. Come back to the Underhill anytime if you want trinkets, or your fortune told. We've men in the brothel too, even a lesser Fae Lord who likes to slum it down here for his sexual kicks with other races."

That caused me to arch an eyebrow in surprise, a Fae Lord in a brothel? While the Fae Lords were almost painful to look at because they were so pretty, I shook my head and said plainly, "Not my cup of tea."

It was his turn to cock an eyebrow and smile appreciatively. "I'll call if they ever get a Fae Lady down there then. It was nice meeting you, Knith Shade."

He sounded almost sad like something might befall me. I just nodded and said, "Thank you for your help, Mac. It was a pleasure." His eye twitched at that. Then as I walked off I said loud enough for him to hear, "Mother, please quantum encrypt my interactions here in Underhill to my bio-signature and pass key only."

She said with a sigh, "Of course, Knith. I'd heed his words

though. I know you and how stubborn and headstrong you can be, but if you pursue this line of questioning, it can be..."

"Whose family crest was that, Mother?"

"Knith..."

"Whose?"

Graz whispered, "House Ashryver."

I startled a nearby woman who smelled like a wildcat shifter with my sharp intake of breath. House Ashryver? But that was Queen Mab's house... There were thousands in her line, but still, that someone in her house was capable doing these abominable things?

I whispered to myself, "I need to go home and think."

As I passed the fortune teller's cabin, she stood in her open door, and called after me, "Beware the sins of the father, Knith of the Enforcer Brigade." She knew who I was? I was almost running by the time I hit the airlock.

Graz whistled low as she shook her head at my predicament while I whispered, "Fuck me sideways and space me naked," as I cycled the door to get back onto the world. We emerged back outside a few minutes later, just as the Day Lights extinguished for nighttime, and the nebula and stars now glowed brightly through the translucent sky glass of the ring past the Trunk.

CHAPTER 5
Here I Go Again

It was a long and restless night. I spent a couple hours reviewing evidence from the prior crime scenes to see if something was missed, and if they aligned with my growing theory. Brass was going to be all up in my case the moment I logged my preliminary case file highlighting what I had learned so far.

I was surprised that Mother hadn't already alerted them to my line of thinking. I was grateful because I knew they would take the case from me and move it up the food chain where it would be quashed for fear of repercussions for our ring if I dared imply any Greater Fae was involved, let alone someone from Queen Mab's own house.

What was I thinking? This could get me reassigned to a D-Ring, or worse... Trunk or Heart patrol. I harrumphed at myself because I knew I couldn't let this go. Every time I closed my eyes I saw the faces of the victims, and if I could find some closure to them or their families, that was what I was going to do.

At least poor Mr. Katan didn't have any next of kin to grieve over his loss. I researched Woodlings and found they were a magical race not connected to the Fae or Fairy. They had the natural ability to collect and store magic inside of them to use at a future time, predominantly for mating, which they did every few hundred years. They were pretty much loners besides that, which was why he was one of only three Woodlings living in our ring and there were only two dozen total on the World.

Mother had already locked down Katan's house and offices here in Irontown by law, and petitioned Judge Greenleaf for a warrant to search the locations before I had even visited the Underhill. The big shaggy Woodling was, of all things, an interior decorator for the richer families of our C-Ring and even some clients up-ring, and was pretty well off himself. I'd have to get to his house by the lake farther up the ring to check it out for anything that may show why he was targeted, other than his ability to pull in and hold magic.

Hmm... I'd have to research the other victims to see if they had any special abilities. But for now, I had woken up a couple hours before Day Lights so headed down from my quarters on the upper level of the barracks, to work out in the gym and think.

I was just in my shorts, tank top and workout shoes, as I decided on a run along the suspended track that circled the gym. I looped a coms earpiece over my ear... I know, I know, why not just get a cybernetic com jack installed like ninety percent of the residents on the world? I was actually unmodded and was sort of proud of the fact, even if it was a little inconvenient at times.

Smiling crookedly I said as I limbered up while a couple more early birds went jogging past, "Mother, cue up something from the anthropological playlist."

"You got it, Knith."

A song called "Here I Go Again", by a group who paid homage

to Fire Wyrms, Whitesnake, started to play and my feet fell with the beat as they sang, "I don't know where I'm going. But I sure know where I've been." When the edgy instrumental kicked in at the hook, I broke into a full out sprint, amazed at the depth of the words for something so ancient. It was like they were speaking my truth.

So I ran, and ran, going over the case in my head. Passing the other runners on the track, some tried to speed up to keep pace with me, but when my heart was pumping like this, and the euphoria of running was driving me, there wasn't an Enforcer that could match my speed, not even the four-legged ones.

Later, the Maretish brothers spotted me on the heavy bags, swinging them at me at awkward angles, or trying to overpower me with direct strikes from the bags. The big brutes were halflings, half-human, half wood elf, and all muscle. And they always enjoyed trying to knock me down.

They've been with the Brigade longer than I have, and they used to run me over with exercises like this, but I kept getting back up again. Improving my speed, strength, and tactics year by year. Watching everyone who wasn't human getting promoted over me.

We did some light sparring to cool down after I spotted them on the weights, not like I'd be much help as they could bench twice what I could.

When I was in the shower, the windows brightened when the Day Lights turned on for the ring. That was my cue. No more procrastinating, time to get to work.

I thanked the guys for the workout and headed back up to my quarters to gear up, and walked right into what could only be described as an aerial battle or light-show from one of the many nearby nightclubs.

Standing there stunned, I saw Graz pushing the books out of the built-in nightstand by my bed and brought my fingers to my lips and whistled shrilly. Three of the five or six glowing Sprites covered their ears and spiraled out of the air to crash spectacularly on the deck plates, another spiraled into a soft explosion of glittery dust in my pillow.

Graz buzzed up to me. "Mab's tits, Knith! A little warning?"

I looked at her incredulously and the items, not mine, strewn all over the place, then the mess at the nightstand. "Graz, what the hells is going on here? And why are you in my quarters? How did you even get in here?"

She shrugged and slapped the back of the head of a male Sprite who buzzed up to ogle me. "Our place now. You owe me."

What!? I voiced my thought "What!?"

Graz shrugged. "We were evicted last night after I left you. Since you stopped me from gathering scrap to sell to pay our rent. We're building our nest in that box thing there beside the bed. You won't even know we're here."

I sputtered out, "You mean sell the stuff you were stealing from the world? Get out or I'll drag you in for trespass."

She flew up between my eyes and crossed her arms obstinately.

"You don't have the balls."

I opened my mouth but she reached out and made a zipping motion over my lips then patted my cheek with her little hand as she streaked off to start making a nest in my nightstand. "Besides, don't you have a case that's going to get you fired or worse to work on?"

Blinking I exhaled loudly. "I don't have time for this. We're going to have words when I get back tonight. Don't get too comfortable."

"Hey, your lips are zipped. Family?" The others buzzed up, a male and female on either side of Graz, hugging her in mid-air as the others, I realized were fledglings, hovered behind them. "Family, this is Knith, the Big that treats us like people, our new landlord. Knith, my family." She pointed at the children and I huffed out in exasperation.

I grumbled under my breath as I stepped behind my changing screen to get into my uniform and armor, "Low... using children to guilt me." She looked so smug just hovering there then she started snapping orders and they all scrambled to comply. I remember reading somewhere that the third gender was boss in their trinary sex race because they were so rare.

I growled when Graz landed on my shoulder as I headed out. She just squeaked, "I've a vested interest in how this case turns out. Besides, I can be useful."

Breathe Knith. I didn't have time to argue. And I had to grin when Graz paled when I asked, "Mother, please compile a list of the

Greater Fae in Mab's house who have medical expertise."

"Knith..."

"I know Mother, just do it." Then I smirked and told both of my unwanted passengers, "Time to visit the A-Rings." I wonder if the mines were nice this time of year in the Heart since that was likely where I was going to end up.

Mother put up three names on my heads up and I waited for the list to either populate more or to start scrolling. When it didn't I asked, "Mother, where are the rest of the names? Are they not listed in the database?"

If an AI could shrug, I got the distinct impression from her tone that she did just that as she supplied, "You asked for a list of people in House Ashryver who had medical expertise. These are they. There are eleven others who are listed as lab techs but wouldn't have the anatomical knowledge or surgical training in other races to have performed the organ harvesting."

Ok, this is what happens when you aren't specific, Mab's line was extensive, and accounted for a full third of the population of Greater Fae on the Leviathan. "I meant, the entire House Ashryver, not just this Ring or Stack."

The Worldship had two forward stacks of four rotating and counter-rotating habitation rings and two matching stacks aft of the Heart. There were three million souls in each stack. Three medical practitioners for even a single ring was ludicrous but you didn't see many Fae Lords outside the A-Rings, and rarely in the B-Rings.

Mother said, "That is the full list, Knith, there are five registered doctors in all the combined Fae houses, the bulk of them in Mab's line."

I chuckled. "Are you doing a diagnostic scan of the core? You're slipping some bits."

The smile melted off my face when Graz squeaked out, "It's true." I blinked at her as she shrugged and said, "The greater Fae don't get sick, and they heal just about any wound in minutes that would kill a member from any other race. They're immortal for all intents and purposes so they don't have any use for doctors."

She sounded resentful and when I prompted with a slight rise of my chin she continued, "Us lesser Fae, we're not pure. So there are a few things that can make us sick, and we heal slow, not stupid slow like Human nulls, but nothing like the Greater Fae Lords and Ladies. And we have just a spark of magic."

She hissed, "They live in the castles they built in the upper rings and the Sprites and Faeries were released into the farmlands down-ring to nest out in the open like animals. They eat like royalty while we scrape together scraps to sell, and live off of food cards that we only get quarter rations with because we're... small." She spat out the last word.

I didn't know what to say to that, and she asked, "Why can't we live in the A-Rings with them? It isn't like we're defective. They even have Pixies and the Fae insects from Old Earth up there, but not us."

The only thing I could think to say was, "I'm sorry?" Then added with a sheepish half-smile as I shrugged and asked, "Life sucks, get used to it?"

She gave the cheesiest of grins back, and sighed now that she got the rant out of her system. She looked much more relaxed now.

I thought out loud. "So... three. That considerably narrows down the list of..."

Mother interrupted. "Don't say suspects, Knith."

I cocked an eyebrow and said instead, "Persons of interest."

Graz asked, "What's the difference?"

Mother supplied dryly, "There isn't one." Then asked, "Wait, why is the Sprite with us?"

I smiled at that. Mother always said things like 'us', like she was walking beside me. Sure she can be overbearing and, heh, mothering at times, but I don't know why the other enforcers find her annoying and wooden.

I'd swear she was actually alive and self-aware if I didn't know any better. Just what did it take for a sophisticated Artificial Intelligence born of a computer system more powerful than two hundred thousand human brains, and magic, to become self-aware? Was it just time? She has certainly had that as we are five thousand years into our journey.

I replied with a shrug, "To hells if I know. She seems to think she has a vested interest in it."

And Mother supplied something I hadn't even thought of.

"Besides Fairies, Sprites are known to be the most curious of races. Similar to Terran cats."

I was squirming and itching as Graz let out a terrified squeak and dove through my open helmet and down the front of my scatter armor. "Cats!?"

I pulled my helmet off and reached down into my cleavage and pulled the squirming Sprite out by her wings. "She just said cats, there aren't any about." Well not that I knew of. They were a favored pet on the mid rings.

She grump mumbled something that sounded suspiciously like "Stupid computer."

I rolled my eyes as I reseated my helmet and then tapped my wrist console. "Control, this is Shade, badge alpha three four eight niner. Send crime scene techs to execute warrant..." I looked up and Mother supplied in my voice "Foxtrot charlie niner niner three slash gamma seven zero." I winked my thanks into the interior helmet cam to her. The satisfied sound I got in return had me picturing her beaming a smile at me.

The response was, "Roger, Shade alpha three four eight niner."

Good, that was one less thing to do today, they would scour the Woodling's office and log everything and perform scans for me to review later. I wanted to be the one to execute the other warrant on Mr. Katan's house. It felt like if I were going to violate the privacy of a dead man's home, I should woman up and do it myself.

Which reminded me. "Mother, can you look for commonalities

between any communications traffic between the victims going back... three weeks prior to the first murder?"

She tsked. "You know I can't do that without a warrant."

I knew that, but I knew she knew the Judge would sign off on it as soon as it cycles through the queue on his desk this morning.

I pouted. "Please?"

She harrumphed. "I don't know why I do these things for you."

I teased. "Because you love me?"

"Against my better judgment."

Graz was just looking at me with a raised eyebrow as we mounted my Tac-Bike. I asked, "What? That's how you deal with a redhead."

"A redhead? It's a computer."

I shrugged and admitted, "I know that, but I always picture her as a testy but helpful redhead in a professional suit behind a desk, pulling strings for my cases."

"I'm not testy."

"I know. I'm just teasing. Don't be testy." I moved my hand up to block the interior helmet cam with a finger as I shook my head at Graz.

Mother said patiently, "You do know I can see you, Knith. I'm everywhere."

I looked up to one of the cameras on the street as we started moving toward the nearest spoke, and I grinned at it as it followed us. "That's why I do it."

I was certifiable, teasing a computer. I thought about that a moment. Watching the cameras watching us as we weaved through the busy morning traffic as people were heading off to work for the day. Well, she was more than a computer, she was actually the Leviathan herself. I found that sort of reassuring in some incomprehensible manner.

We pulled into the spoke transit terminal lot and I mag-locked the bike and headed in. The trams ran every three minutes during rush hour. We were standing alone in the back of the tram as everyone gave me a wide birth as usual. Did everyone view us Enforcers as that bad? I know that whenever we respond to an emergency, they seemed awfully glad to see us. Was it just the authority they didn't like? Didn't they understand that we, in essence, worked for them? You know, the whole public servant thing?

I sighed and got out of my head. It was an old scab I liked to pick at year after year. But truth be told, I can't think of doing any other job on the world. I loved protecting the people on my ring.

As Gravity increased to almost one Earth gravity as we passed through the B-Ring, letting off the majority of the riders, we continued on up into the high gravity of the A-Ring. I was glad I trained in one point two five G whenever I could, or I would have felt sluggish as we stepped off of the tram with two lesser fae.

I took a deep breath at the doors and steeled myself as I stepped out into paradise. From the raised platform I looked out over the sprawling forests of the A-Ring, with the lakes and rivers flowing through it, gleaming spires sticking up in clumps, and old villages of stone and wood, built along the river's edge.

There was color everywhere punctuating the green space that they say was a piece of the old world. Flowers bloomed everywhere, and colorful birds and insects buzzed around the treetops. I even caught sight of one of the herds of deer that roamed freely through this almost alien world to the other lower rings in each stack.

I inhaled deeply the heavy, unprocessed air. The forests themselves provided most of the breathable atmosphere up here, they had emergency processors that have never run, except to circulate the air in the bulkhead buildings and corridors.

The air was as sweet and heavy as a dream and I smiled almost involuntarily. Get with it Knith, these are Fae lands, everything here is designed to lull you into a sense of tranquility and let your guard down. The Fae Lords and Ladies are born manipulators, and masters of deception.

Still, I took a moment to appreciate the sheer beauty and artistry of the ring, as the misty gray clouds high overhead started dropping a cool, misty rain down on us. I loved the rain when the moisture in the air in most of the rings reached saturation levels and the rain came down. I always got the impression that it washed away all the grime of the lower rings, cleansing them and us, if just for a little while.

I took my helmet off again, as Graz crawled under my collar again, shielding her head with her arms. I looked up and closed my eyes to let the cool droplets hit my face. I know I was here for more pressing business, but I took this moment to bask in one of the few amazing moments on the world.

I inhaled deeply, feeling refreshed, shaking out my wet hair as I placed my helmet back on, tucking the dark locks back inside. "Come on Graz, get out."

I felt her shaking her head. "Nuh-uh. Not until that nasty stuff stops falling."

"The rain? It's just water."

"You know what it does to our wings? Makes a nasty paste with the dust until it dries. I'm ok in here."

I rolled my eyes, of course, she wouldn't enjoy one of the miracles of the Worldship. Unfortunately, the rain wouldn't last long. The Old Earth Fae talk of the Open Air, where rains covered thousands and sometimes millions of square miles and could go on for days. But as large as the rings are, being big enough to generate their own weather, the volume is the tiniest fraction of the atmosphere in Open Air.

This all means... the rain trickled off into a mist then stopped altogether as we made our way down the powered spiraling walk down to ground level. My Sprite stowaway crawled out, sitting on my helmet rim next to my jaw, looking up, before deciding it was safe and zipped out to hover beside me as I walked along the dirt path to the terminal exit.

It is said that all the dirt from the upper rings is actually soil from Earth itself, instead of the unusable regolith leftovers from mining the Heart, and compost used to make the green spaces in the lower rings. I bounced on my toes as I stepped through the ornate gates. Was this what walking on the Ground was like?

I looked across the smallish settlement built around the spoke for trade and commerce, though not many Down-Ringers like me traded with the Fae, knowing that any deals made would weigh heavily in the favor of the Fae. The ones who did were usually the ones who wished to be in good favor with those who really held the power on the world, both figuratively and literally.

The main reason the Fae are basically in charge is that without them, the Worldship would not be possible. Though every square inch of the hull was covered in photovoltaic paint that harvested every photon and even cosmic radiation from the stars at ninety-eight percent efficiency, and the fission reactors run with a dwindling fissionable fuel supply from the rare metals mined from the Heart. They supply a fraction of the power it takes to run the Leviathan.

Most of the energy to run the core systems and the massive World-Drives comes from the Fae. Specifically the Fae artifacts of power, the source of all their magic away from the Earth. Power so vast it is difficult to comprehend. And only the Greater Fae Lords and Ladies, under the orders of Queen Mab herself, can extract the power safely in the Chamber of the Artifacts, the Ka'Ifinitum.

So even though we have a president, and are a democracy, and the Fae pretend to be governed by the laws of the world... they are the ones with the true power. And here I was, going to question Mab's own, following my suspicions. Am I crazy? Maybe. But I have to bring the souls of the victims some sort of peace, some sort of closure.

"Mother? Some transportation?" I really should have just ridden my Tac-Bike up the spoke's transportation lane, but during the stop and go rush hour it would have taken thirty or forty minutes to get here. At least I could have ridden it up here since only non-emission and non-ground-contact vehicles are allowed.

"Look up."

I looked up and a sleek dart-shaped transport, that looked to be made of a single seamless piece of iridescent material which looked suspiciously like a pearl, soundlessly swooped down under a flock of white birds I think were doves, to hover just a foot away from me as a door slid up from the seamless body.

I snicked my visor down and zoomed in on where the door had just slid up and magnified almost to the molecular level and I couldn't detect the seam between the door and whatever pocket it slid up into. Overlays came up on demand and the whole vessel shimmered as I took in the intricate spell work virtually cocooning it.

I whistled low as I stepped inside flicking my visor back up again. "Damn, the Fae do good work." I was sure the vessel wasn't powered by any mundane means, I instinctively knew it was pure magic.

The door sealed itself, and I didn't bother looking for a seam, knowing I wouldn't find one. Then I snorted at this sleek luxurious transport. Why didn't we have anything like this down-ring? I answered my own question... separation of the classes, Knith.

I looked at the three names in my peripheral and pointed at one, asking, "Why does Aurora ring a bell?"

Graz zipped up to my nose putting her hands on either side of it as she stared expectantly into my eyes, "Ummm..."

Mother chuckled and prompted, "Mab's daughter?"

I muttered, "Oh space me..." Princess Aurora? She was one of the Fae medical experts? Suicide. I was committing career suicide here. I could turn around now and move the murder into the cold case files and walk away.

I sighed and looked at the address and balked yet again. Of course. I said in resignation to the vessel since there were no controls in it as I stared vacantly out the window, "Mab's palace please." Then we rose up and silently sliced through the air along the treetops then started climbing rapidly through the sparse air traffic as I sat to think, mumbling, "May as well start at the top, Knith. I mean, what could possibly go wrong?"

The Sprite hovered back to study me and prompted carefully, "You're not backing down, are you?"

I shook my head as Mother nattered in the background under her nonexistent breath to what I assumed was herself, "She doesn't know what's good for her. By all means, get yourself relegated to ore duty, don't listen to me."

Graz grinned like a loony goof as she said, "I knew there was a reason I liked you. You're not like the other Bigs. I mean, you're big and dumb and a null and everything, but I guess you're ok."

I snorted. "Remember that when you're down in the Heart sorting rocks with me."

When Mother harrumphed over me making jokes about what was likely my probable future, I realized something. The epiphany that Mother... was afraid of the Fae. They alone had the ability to turn her off, as they supplied her with the power to run all her systems. They could in effect, kill her if they cut power. Could an AI be afraid? Was it real or simulated fear? I wasn't sure. Isn't self-preservation one of the signs of sentience?

I reassured, "It's all going to be ok, Mother. I mean, it has to right? Only good can come from doing the right thing, otherwise, what's the point?" Both of them were silent.

I turned to look out the windows that were so clear, it was impossible to tell if they were really there. We were a couple thousand feet up now. High enough I could actually see the complex honeycomb grid-work that held the massive, multilayered, clear armored panels of the sky with the unaided eye. Every fourth honeycomb in the central strips of the ring's torus, a Day Light, was glowing brightly.

I took a moment to appreciate the monumental engineering feat that was the Leviathan. And what a herculean task it must have been to build her on orbit over a thousand-year period. I voiced that. "The world is kind of amazing, isn't she?"

Mother chirped out in a pleased and perky tone, "Thank you."

Graz replied, "And modest."

Then I was gasping, I had never seen Mab's palace, Ha'real, except in holos and pictures, and neither did it justice. With a central pointed tower of opalescent white that stretched almost a half-mile high, with other lesser spires surrounding it, extending half that height melding in with the bulkhead on one side and stretching out to the lake in the middle of the ring, low structures were arranged at the base to create a walled courtyard of green that ran the whole length of the palace, and waterfalls fell into the courtyard from big jagged rocks that melded into the bulkhead beside the towers there.

Were those big rocks... were they what they called 'mountains', from all the tales of Old Earth? I'd have to look it up. But whatever they were, it was a breathtaking sight. I saw the shimmering dome of the massive wards set up around the palace and contemplated the sheer amount of power the casters must have had to create something so massive.

I saw flocks of birds effortlessly swooping in and out of the wards, no threat so unaffected. Then the transport slowed as we reached the shimmering dome and I caught myself holding my breath as we sank into it. The power sparked off of my scatter armor, which would be useless against a spell of this magnitude anyway, and I felt the magic probing my body and mind.

Disliking the invasion of privacy, I pushed back, thinking, "Get off of me!" I could feel it recoil then it was gone and I was gasping out to the ward, "She's with me, let her go," when I heard a muffled squeak. Graz was spasming on the deck of the vessel, looking like she was being constricted by some invisible snake. Then it released her.

I was sort of upset at that. It seems that even though she was a lesser Fae, her larger cousins actually did treat Sprites as vermin like she had ranted about. I... was not a fan of the ward. Not like I had any say in it at all.

As I scooped up my exhausted looking companion, she squinted one eye at me as she rode on my hand until I deposited her on my shoulder. "Did Mab's ward just listen to you?"

Mab made that ward? I had assumed it was a collective of the most powerful Fae who had constructed it, not just one. Was the Queen truly that powerful? I really didn't want to know, and I was going to go out of my way to avoid her if I could.

I shrugged. "Since our visit was unannounced, I think the ward reacted poorly. But I assume that once it determined I was an Enforcer, it decided to let me through. And since I said you were with me, it let you through."

She shook her head. "You talk like magic can reason." I shrugged. I was talking out of my ass since I didn't have a clue why the ward backed off when I pushed against it, but I talked a good game, right?

I saw guards assembling at a small landing pad in the courtyard, near some soaring arched doors of the seamless construction of the palace. They had long pikes that I knew were more than just physically dangerous, they were channels for their magics, making them twice as deadly. The Queen's guard were the only people outside the Enforcer Brigade allowed to carry powered weapons. It was a concession made back before the Exodus.

We landed and the door slid open. I stepped out and knew better than to look the guards in the face. That's how Humans got enthralled, the beauty of the greater Fae was more than the Human mind could comprehend. It is how all the Humans in the fables and cautionary tales about Faerie and its people became enslaved by the whims of the Fae.

I didn't know if it was true or the embellishments of adults trying to scare the young, but I didn't want to put it to the test. I had never looked into the faces of the few Greater Fae I had met, and wasn't going to start now as I stared at the chin of the guard who stepped forward, her armor of gleaming light that could only be Ethereal clung to her lithe and enticing form, as her straight white hair that glinted of silver and purple highlights flowed over her shoulders. The skin of her long, feminine neck and sculpted chin looked unreal.

Too smooth, too flawless, like porcelain just begging to be touched.

"State your business at Ha'real..." She almost spat out, "Human." Breaking the spell of my appreciation of her.

I sighed and straightened, looking at her cheek so our eyes would be level, I wasn't going to be caught looking down in her presence. I was the law, she was a glorified bodyguard, and I didn't like her attitude. "Brigade business, step aside."

She moved her pike to below my chin. "Not until you state your business with the Winter Lady."

I grabbed the pike and moved it away from my face, gripping the bladed end of it, the spells on it sparking and scattering on my gauntlet. "Unless you want to be bound by law for threatening an Enforcer of the Brigade, you'll get your little stick out of my face..." I added, indicating I held rank, "Citizen."

We both knew I couldn't do it, it would get caught up in the political machine, the charges dropped for some technicality, then my C-Ring would suffer unfortunate malfunctions of the water or air processing systems, or temperature control until the Fae felt we had been punished enough for my audacity. I wouldn't be the most popular person in the ring after that.

I could feel her eyes trying to bore into me and I smiled and said, "I'm not here for Mab." Purposefully omitting Queen to ruffle their feathers. I figure I was already in the shit, hip-deep, might as well go for a swim. I chanced looking into her eyes without taking in her face.

Gods, they were a beautiful ice blue like none I'd ever seen before, but I concentrated on the pupils so I wouldn't be tempted to look at her face. "I'm here on an official investigation, I have questions for Aurora of House Ashryver."

She studied me, her eyes intense and I smirked internally when she blinked first and looked away. "And you, of course, have an appointment? The princess is a very busy woman, an important woman."

I patted the badge on my hip. "Here's my appointment. Now please, move aside so I can do my job, or I will bind you by law."

She said in challenge, "You wouldn't."

I shrugged and said, "Try me," as I pulled out a mag-band and reached for her hand. "Delphine of House Kryn, captain of the Queen's Guard, I hereby..."

There were a dozen pikes at my throat, and the woman asked as she held up a halting hand and the pikes withdrew, "You know who I am?"

"Of course. Now, are you going to let me do my job or do we do this the hard way?" I moved one leg slightly back to a fighting stance and readied myself.

She was silent for a long moment, then she started to laugh, she was wiping tears from her cheek as she gasped out, "You'd really take on a score of the Queen's finest? A human?" Then she composed herself and said as I caught her cocking a brow in my peripheral vision as I concentrated on the tracking of the guards who were now surrounding me, "Oh, you're serious."

Again I said as I wiggled the mag-band between us and repeated, "Try me."

She asked almost conversationally, "And what ring do you hail from, Enforcer?" I caught the implied threat but didn't waver.

I said, "The, 'last chance to let me past before I haul your pretty little ass in' ring."

I caught the blades of two guards who took umbrage with me threatening their commander and went to put their blades at my throat again, but I was waiting. I slipped back and grabbed the shafts of the two incoming pikes and yanked forward, using the guards' own momentum to drive through the space I had been and jammed the points of the pikes up under the chins of each other, stopping an inch from their skin.

Silence fell in the entire courtyard, then Delphine started chuckling, and the others followed after an awkward moment. "Duly noted, you may be more capable than you appear. What did you say your name was?"

She mumbled into her wrist console too low for me to hear.

And I asked, "Who me? I'm Nobody." I locked eyes with her again and she tried to read me, and I saw the confusion when she saw no lie in my eyes. Heh, first time being named Shade worked out for me.

She cocked her head, listening to something then nodded to herself as she stepped aside, and made a sweeping ushering motion.

"You may enter, a guide will meet you at the doors, but mark my words, the Princess is too busy to see you."

I shoved the pikes away and the men made unappreciative grunts as they stood at attention with the rest. Mother was whispering in my ear, "Are you crazy, Knith? You couldn't have fought them off. They're Fae. Maybe one on one, but..." I gave thin air a plaintive look and she stopped.

Delphine said, "Your pet needs to stay here."

Graz zipped up into the air and flew straight at the captain, screeching, "Pet? I'm nobody's pet you overgrown pile of beetle dung!" And she stopped in mid-air, a hair's breadth from the razor-sharp pike blade that was now in front of her.

She reached out and tapped her thumb on the point and pulled back to suck the blood off the cut such casual contact had made. Then she back flapped her way toward me, stating, "On second thought..."

I just pinched her wings from the air and sat her firmly on my shoulder. "This Sprite is a material witness and she comes with me."

The Captain mock bowed at me and as I stepped past I started to say, "Th..." Then I clamped my mouth shut, feeling the anticipation in her. Oh, hells no was I going to thank her. She'd just love to have me in her debt. I decided to be the bigger person and instead offered as I walked past, "You do your station and your Queen proud." I could feel her beaming with pride as I walked, perhaps a little quickly, away.

I heard her calling out, "Maybe another day, Enforcer. I find your lack of self-preservation... refreshing."

I snorted in spite of myself and just held up my middle finger as I walked, without looking back, to the chuckling of the guards. Gods, they were just as bad as the men in the Brigade.

To my surprise, a Wood Elf was waiting at the fifty-foot tall arched doors, back against the huge frame in an aloof manner. He cocked a brow, "Oh... you're human?"

I sighed and asked nobody in particular, "What is this? Dump on humans day?"

To a one, this elf, Graz, and even Mother, said in unison, "Every day is dump on Humans day." Why the fuck was I smiling? It was an old and tired joke.

I asked, "I suppose you're my guide?"

He nodded and offered a hand. "J'real Leafwalker. They were sending a maid, but I just had to see the Enforcer who had the balls to challenge Delphine."

I shook his hand and said, "Shade, and this is Graz."

He looked confused and said, "You know, in Old Faerie, Shade means..."

"Just shut up and guide if you're going to guide."

I liked his smirk. The man didn't take himself seriously. He asked conversationally, "What brings an officer from the Enforcer's Brigade to Ha'real to speak with Rory?"

Rory? He could be so familiar with Princess Aurora that he

could call her Rory? I cocked a brow and the dashing Elf wiggled his brows. "Someday, I will win her heart. Mark my words, then the two most powerful houses on the world would be one."

I blinked. "Wait, wait, wait... you're the J'real? Of House Thule of the Elves?" I appraised the pretty man with his roguish appearance. I may prefer women, but I still knew sexy. He had it in spades.

He winked, then looped an arm in mine as he guided me through an endless maze of corridors, going up and down levels as he just made small talk while skillfully trying to coax information from me. The man was good and I liked him in spite of myself. It dawned on me that I was talking to a prince. I almost snorted at that because he was so, well, un-princely and mostly genuine except for what he thought was his sly attempts to find out why I needed to talk to the woman he was apparently romantically pursuing.

I was thoroughly and completely lost by the time we arrived at a set of doors that looked like any of the other hundreds we passed, and he grasped a handle and pulled one open for me as he bowed low and made an ushering flourish with his hand. "My lady."

I muttered to him through a smile, "You're not as charming as you think you are, buster."

He stood and followed me into a huge open office space, assuring me as he scratched the tip of one of his pointed ears, "Oh but I have it on good authority that I am."

The cavernous space was empty except a single nondescript desk that looked to be made of a single rectangular block of white stone. There was a Fae woman sitting in the chair behind it. I started to panic. What was I supposed to do? I've never met royalty before, present company excluded of course, but J'real didn't count.

I awkwardly bowed and said, "Princess Aurora."

The woman was startled and screamed and fell off her chair and I started to rush forward when she bounced up from the floor like she was on springs, and spun to the door behind her, smoothing down her white skirt, starting to bow as she asked, "Where?" Then she relaxed and looked between the door and me, narrowing her eyes. "Dirty trick that."

Oh, gods, I was smiling at the awkward woman as she attempted to regain her dignity, adjusting the lapels on her stark white blouse.

J'real offered, "Enforcer Shade, Nyx, secretary and personal assistant to Princess Aurora."

I strode forward, hand out, feeling embarrassed as I told her, "I'm so sorry to have startled you, Nyx. It's nice to meet you. I'm here on official business to speak with Aurora of House Ashryver. Is she in?"

She blinked at me as I looked at the cute dimple on her flawlessly porcelain cheek, not daring to gaze at her face. Then she looked back at the door. "Nice to meet you. Umm... I don't really know." She leaned an ear against the door and supplied, "She's always coming and going..."

I grinned and prompted helpfully, "Has she come out today?" I was already loving this woman. In all my imaginings I've never pictured a Greater Fae as being awkward and almost scatterbrained. But with just my first impression of the woman, I came to the startling revelation that Fae came in all shapes and sizes just like regular people.

I placed my ear on the door too, then J'real joined us. Nyx whispered, "I don't know, she uses the back door, I've never really, you know, umm... met the Princess."

I pulled back from the door and blinked at her in surprise. "But you're her secretary and personal assistant."

She nodded and sighed. "Yet she does everything herself. Very hands-on that one. But mark my words, one day she'll need someone to take a message, and I'll be there to message the hells out of it."

I smiled fondly at the woman and patted her shoulder. "I'm sure you will."

Then I prompted, "Mind if I go in?"

I started pulling the two doors open and just strode in as she started to squeak in protest.

CHAPTER 6
Bohemian Rhapsody

My armor sparked and heated and I pushed my way through the gelatin-like thick and tacky ward as the magic tried to stick to me. My face prickled at a million stings as the ward tried to take hold, then I was through. Nyx calling out behind me, "You can't!"

A woman stood in what could only be described as a laboratory, tech den, or possibly an alchemist parlor. Maybe all of the above due to all the equipment I was seeing.

Then I drew my MMGs and fired at the other woman in the corner who was starting to cast on me, the weapon whirred and reloaded as the Fae fell to the floor convulsing at the electric charge that was dampening her magics and concentration as the tiny pronged dart shocked her.

I didn't even look at the man in the opposite corner who just froze, his hands halfway up to start his own casting. I said to him without looking as I took in the tall woman in the middle of the room in a long white robe, who was holding onto a large beaker of fluid, "I wouldn't. I can pull the trigger faster than you can utter the first syllable. Stand down, I'm with the Brigade."

Then to the woman, I bowed as graciously as I could manage while holding two MMGs pointed toward the two magic slingers. "Princess Aurora, I'm Knith Shade, Enforcer, here to beg audience."

I didn't know how she would react, but I didn't expect how she did as she snorted, placed the beaker on the counter in front of her, and removed silken white gloves as she said, "Knith Shade. Quite an entrance." Her voice almost had an actual taste to me, of sweet honey with a bit of spice, it sent a not unpleasant shiver down my spine.

Then she made a flick of her finger toward the man, and he dropped his hands then went rushing over to the woman who had stopped convulsing on the deck, without any regard to the weapon I had trained on him. He helped the stunned woman to her feet and moved quickly out a door in the wall I swear hadn't been there a moment before.

The Princess sat on the corner of the counter and said, "Knith Shade... why do I know that name?" Then she shook her head and said in almost delighted amusement, "You're... Human." It was surprise, not derision. She looked at me and narrowed her eyes in my peripheral vision as I focused on the alchemy rack just over her shoulder. Then she looked to the corners her guards or whatever had been. "How did you see my guards? They were behind a don't look here that I cast myself. And you got past my ward on the door."

I rolled my eyes and looked down at myself as I spun the weapons and holstered them simultaneously. By the gods, was I showing off for her? "Brigade armor, standard-issue, spelled to let us see magic and through bullshit."

I blushed at that and apologized, "I'm sorry. I shouldn't be so vulgar around a lady. I'm just on edge after meeting the Queen's guard."

She snorted again. "A lady? Please, tell my mother that. I like your bluntness." Then she smirked and said in a sly tone, "If only there really were a spell to see through bullshit. But then we Fae would lose our advantage."

She looked past me and made a distressed sound. "Oh, and who did you bring with you?"

I looked back to see both Graz and J'real frozen in the doorway, caught up in an immobility ward, the Sprite's eyes wide in shock, the elf's mouth open like he was about to speak. I saw frost gathering on them. Aurora was the daughter of the Winter Lady, so her magics must be similar to her mother's, rooted in a season the ship emulated on only the upper two rings of the stacks for a quarter of the year.

She flicked a finger and Graz fell through the doorway and almost hit her face on the deck plates before she arrested her fall with her frantically flapping wings in the heavier gravity. Frost sloughed off of her and onto the deck.

She spotted me and buzzed my way as I said, "Princess Aurora, may I present to you, Graz, Sprite of C-Ring, Beta-Stack. My... umm... consultant."

Graz's eye widened and she almost went into free fall as she dove for the deck and landed at the last moment to get on her knees and laid herself out, arms outstretched in supplication. Her voice squeaked out in awe, "Highness."

The woman strode forward as she wondered aloud, "A Human,

and you consort with lesser Fae?" She chuckled and looked to the empty corner, "And tilt at windmills." What did that even mean?

She scooped Graz up to sit on her hand, and with her other, she reached in to straighten the Sprite's tunic as she said formally, "It is a pleasure to meet you, Graz, Sprite of C-Ring, Beta-Stack."

Ok, the look of pleasure on the Sprite's face from being acknowledged by a Princess of the Fae, looked to be an almost sexual thing, which had me blushing and looking elsewhere. A dreamy-eyed Graz buzzed drunkenly to my shoulder, a goofy look on her face.

Then her attention was on me after I made sure Graz wouldn't slip off and land on her dazed butt. "So Enforcer, you said something about begging?" She shot me a sly smile at that, then added, "What brings you to my workshop at the risk of gaining disfavor with my mother's cronies? There's not been an Enforcer in Ha'real since... well there has never been an Enforcer in the palace."

That, was not a veiled threat like the captain had used. And it was the truth. I mean it had to be since greater Fae couldn't physically lie. It was a curse or something on their race, something to do with their missing King, Oberon. I knew plenty of Enforcers have been on the A-Rings, hells I have, but apparently not in Ha'real. Her words and tone seemed to disapprove of the way the Fae brandished their power to punish those who displeased them.

I was going to answer, then paused and looked back at the door, where J'real was actually turning a bit blue as icicles were forming on his eyebrows.

"Umm... what about him?"

She smirked and shrugged. "He wasn't invited. Always trying to curry my affection, maybe this will cool his libido a touch."

Ok, she was funny, I'd give her that. We shared crooked smiles and she rolled her eyes and flicked a finger, and he fell forward, halfway through saying my name.

He stumbled, but with elf-quick reflexes, recovered, shivered, and lifted a finger as he started to speak. She stopped him. "Not a word Jay. This delightful Enforcer, who does not fear the Winter Lady's wrath, has business with me."

She really believed I didn't fear her mother? Queen Mab scared the shit out of me, then I'm sure she'd scare the shit out of my shit. I knew the stories of the ice sculptures of the beautiful men and women who had displeased her, forever worshiping her beauty in inanimate frozen frustration forever.

A morbid part of me wondered if I could sneak a peek in the receiving hall to see if those rumors were true. But even if there were ice statues there, were they actually people or were they just sculptures placed there to perpetuate the rumors?

He bowed with a flourish and said, "As you wish, my la... mmph." His mouth was sealed with a layer of ice, and I had never even seen her cast.

She pointed at the open doors. "Out, Jay. I said, not a word."

He actually punched his own face and the ice broke, he winked first at her, then me, before bowing to both of us and backing out of the room with a roguish smirk on his face. He hopped up to sit on Nyx's desk and pretended he couldn't hear us, as Nyx slowly sat back down at her empty desk.

The Princess sighed to me and confided under her breath, "Men. Always with the courting."

I nodded in understanding. "But as far as J'real, at least he's charming."

She chuckled out in pure amusement, "Then you court him. He's the best of the lot, it's just that... I see him more as a friend."

"Ouch!"

She didn't even look back, just pointed at him and he held his hands up.

I said plainly so there was no misunderstanding, "Not my cup of tea." She cocked an exquisitely sculpted eyebrow.

"Ouch!"

And before I could stop my traitorous mouth, I was teasing, "Not that I'd want another woman's cast-offs anyway."

This time both Aurora and I chimed out in unison with the Elf prince, "Ouch!"

She tipped her head back and laughed a silvery laugh that resonated through my entire body as I froze when she placed a long delicate hand with nails that looked to be perfectly manicured... ice? On my arm to steady herself. Her skin looked so... smooth, so unblemished and perfect, I resisted the urge to touch it to make sure she was real.

I had to double-take when I saw the Elf leaning over to play with Nyx's hair as he said, "Alas, I'll have to find another to woo. Nyx, has anyone ever told you that you've the loveliest lavender eyes?"

The poor Fae girl was just about melting into a puddle in front of our eyes. The Princess explained, "That one's a helpless flirt."

Then she let go of my arm and stepped away, back to whatever experiment she was working on as she prompted, "I'm sure you didn't come to exchange dating tips. You wished to speak with me, and that you've made it this far, I'm assuming it is quite important."

My smile dropped. And I re-centered myself. Get with the program, Knith, this is how the Fae entrap the unwary. She's a suspect until you clear her, so act like it.

"Miss Ashryver, I'm investigating a string of murders down-ring, and had a few questions that maybe you can help me with." I looked up to her sculpted cheekbone, careful not to take her face in.

She set her beaker down again and frowned, all the playful tones out of her voice as she asked, "So it's Miss Ashryver now is it?" Then she looked almost excited as realization dawned. "Oh, how exciting, I'm a suspect." Then she added as I looked at her like she was a few shovels short of an ore cart. "Please, ask your questions Enforcer Shade." She looked as if she were seconds away from clapping excitedly in front of her chest.

I sighed then said, "As I said, I'm currently investigating a string of murders. Unauthorized organ harvesting to be precise. I wanted to know if you knew any of these men."

With a flick, I accessed her extensive network of holo-projectors, and pictures of the victims bloomed between us. She looked at them and shook her head. "No, no, no, no. And yes. That's Reiner, everyone knows him, he's the interior designer for everyone who's anyone."

Ok, Fae answer. No could mean anything with a Fae, like no she didn't know them before she harvested their organs and left them to die, or no she's never seen them before. And she didn't really answer definitively about Mr. Katan, she could just know him from the commercials on the waves.

I sighed and rephrased as I put up the crime scene photos beside each. "So you are saying that you have never met the first four? And Mr. Katan, did you know him by reputation or have you had dealings with him?"

It was all I could do to look away from her smiling lips, back to her cheekbone. Her lips were full and inviting with a tinge of blue that played off her almost stark white skin to make her look like some sort of ice sculpture herself.

She chuckled. "Not your first time dealing with the Fae I see. What do I get for playing this game?"

Shaking my head I assured her, "Peace of mind that you did the right thing in helping to bring a killer to justice, and peace for the victims and their families."

She contemplated that, then shook her head. "All noble pursuits, and tempting, but a shameless attempt to play on my morality. So as you seem to know that isn't our way, and because of that, instead of freely answering as my conscience would have had me do, how about I answer each of your questions, and you answer questions in turn as payment."

Always dealing, the Fae. But what profit could she make with me answering questions? What questions could she possibly have for me? Or was she stalling because I was on to her? I exhaled in exasperation and nodded. "Within reason. And if you refuse to answer any, I may have to bind you by law and bring you down to Central to ask again."

This seemed to please her, especially the threat. Then she asked as she shifted in my vision again, "Why won't you look at me?"

I chuckled. "You know why."

She sighed. "You're afraid I'll glamour you? One, it doesn't work that way. Well except for the Winter and Summer Ladies. We have to will it to enthrall you. And two, I will not do so to you unless you ask it of me. I cannot lie so you know I speak the truth."

Against my better judgment, but bolstered by the fact she had plainly said she would not do it to me, and she could not lie, I looked up and caught my breath. Aurora was perhaps the most beautiful creature I had ever laid eyes upon, and her doll-like features, flawless skin, flowing white and silver hair, with those sublime pointed ears sticking through her locks, coupled with bright violet eyes had me gaping at her. But to my relief I didn't feel my free will slipping away, she was just that breathtaking.

She cocked her head and smiled in a way that had the attention of all my most interesting spots. "There, that's better. Now we can take measure of each other as we spar. Your eyes are gorgeous, I've never seen a human with brown eyes which had that lilac ring around them. Varied species interbreeding?"

What? Wait. Wasn't I supposed to be asking the questions? My cheeks were burning now. I'm not supposed to be attracted to a person of interest. Mother whispered in my ear, "Knith, are you alright? Your heart rate is elevated." I typed on the virtual console. "Not now, Mother!"

The smirk on Aurora's face was priceless, snapping me out of it, and I said, "Don't get full of yourself, woman, you're not as pretty as you think." Lies. All lies.

Then I said, "One hundred percent, red-blooded human."

She arched an exquisitely sculpted brow at that, then inclined her head.

"I owe you an answer now. Yes, I have had professional dealings with Mr. Katan." She leaned back almost suggestively against the counter.

I blinked it away, she knew exactly what she was doing to me. I had stupidly shown weakness when I basically admitted I preferred women and Fae are quite fluid in their sexuality. I'm sure she saw it as a tool to get what she wanted out of me.

But then she suddenly stood straight and stepped up to the

projections and enlarged the wounds on each of the victims. She started tracing them with her fingers, eyes wide and studying. "How were these incisions made?"

Ah to the meat of the matter. I exhaled, pulled my eyes from the ten thousand chit white heels she was wearing which I caught sight of under her gown when she strode forward. The price of them helpfully displayed in my peripheral by Mother. Why would I care what they cost? Sometimes Mother can be weird.

Then again, maybe my eyes lingered on them longer than was professional and she tried to anticipate what I was looking at. The silly AI knew my pathetic bank balance, and impractical shoes like that would set me back three month's pay.

I was startled out of my thoughts when a hand rested on my arm. "Are you alright, Enforcer Shade?"

I said absently, as my blood chilled when I saw the talon shaped Ionga ring on her thumb, "Knith." Space me, that put a damper on my libido instantly. Circumstantial Knith, many Fae wear Ionga rings, remember?

She smiled and said, "Then Rory, please. You were stating how these incisions were made."

Tonelessly I supplied, "I didn't say. But do you recognize this?"

My attention snapped to her violet eyes to see the reaction when I flicked the projection of the scalpel up between us. She didn't even blink when she said simply, "Yes." Oh, she was good.

I narrowed my eyes and added, "Care to expound upon that? Do you know who owns it?"

She shook her head, tapping her lower lip. "Those are two more questions, that isn't how this game is played. You'll have to be more specific in the future."

I was suddenly feeling like she was a predator, and I was the prey. Could I see her being a woman who could kill these people in cold blood to steal organs from them? What could be the motive? To sell them on the black market? She had enough money to buy every person on the world and still have more money than the gods left over.

She was going through the data on the wounds a line at a time, like she was absorbing it, or was she a killer admiring her own work? She circled the other way around the projections as I circled toward her. She smirked like she was enjoying this game of cat and mouse. Maybe this really was a game to her. The bored rich girl who was doing this for the thrill? No... that didn't track.

Her question surprised me.

"Do you know what all the missing organs have in common? Knith?"

I blinked and admitted, "I was researching that, but haven't had time to dig deeper yet. Why, do you?"

"Yes. I do."

Doh! I facepalmed and dragged my hand down my face at wasting a question. Graz said out the side of her mouth, "Good going, genius." I made a show of double zipping her lips and she sat back, crossing her arms over her chest with a harrumph.

Aurora asked her question, "When was the first killing?"

I wasn't going to put the whole file up for her to see, so I read off the first date.

I looked at her expectantly since she already knew my question. She nodded and said, "Each of these races, are the most rare of every preternatural species on the world. They all have the distinction of not being Fae, but still being able to either hold magic or absorb it. Your killer has been removing the organs from them that allow this ability. There is just one anomaly to the apparent pattern."

Ok, that made me sit up and take notice. So there was some sort of connection between the killings, maybe... I said to the air, "Mother, can you start building a predictive model, utilizing this new information?"

She replied in a rather good mood so all could hear, "On it, Knith."

Rory blinked at that. "Was that, Mother? I've never heard her emote before."

I said quickly, "Yes. My turn."

She realized her mistake and laughed that silvery laugh as she pointed at me accusingly and said, "You would make a fine Fae, Knith." She seemed to like to use my name. Wait, a lot of magic was tied to knowing someone's true name. But though Knith Shade was the name given to me. I knew my true name, what I called myself in my heart, and that wasn't it. So if that was her game...

I wish she'd stop smiling at me. I absently wondered if that glossy sheen of blue on her lips was actually ice. Turning back to the projections I asked, "You say you recognize the surgical instrument, do you know who owns it, and as part of the questions, if so, then who?"

She shrugged and smiled winningly at me like I had just asked the right question. She chirped out like it was a prize, "Me." She strode over to what looked like some sort of dissection table and grabbed a canvas roll as I lowered one hand to rest on an MMG. The probable murder weapon was hers, and she admitted it.

She unrolled the canvas on the counter and a dozen gleaming silver surgical instruments were displayed, sticking out of little pockets in the canvas, but right in the middle was an empty pocket. She asked, "Do you have it? It has been missing for some time now."

I smiled at her and she made a pained look, then she shook a finger at me as she smiled as I said simply, "Yes."

I still had some questions that needed clarification, but I was starting to suspect something more was going on here than what it all looked like. I had to do my due diligence first. Establish her relationship to the decedents and get an alibi, which my gut was starting to tell me that she just might have, otherwise why would she be playing this game and why admit to owning the murder weapon.

Instead, what I asked was an inane, "Who has access to this

room and those implements?"

She answered very specifically, with urging in her eyes to pick up on the exact terminology she chose, "Only myself, my two palace guards, the Winter Lady of course, and Oberon's children."

She had stressed 'Oberon's children', was she trying to tell me something? She prompted with her eyes. Wait, was she under some sort of geas and couldn't speak freely about something? That was the worst kind of magic, a geas affected your mind and sometimes even your body to prevent you from doing or saying something.

She looked hopeful as she saw me putting things together. Ok, Mab had thirteen children, who all begat thirteen children, and so on.

But Oberon. Oberon was the lover of the Summer Lady, Queen Titania, before the world of Faerie was torn asunder, and when the dust settled there were two great houses, Seelie and Unseelie, Summer and Winter, light and dark. Then Oberon had to choose, and he believed he could tame the wild and volatile Mab for the good of all Faerie and unite the houses, so wed the Winter Lady to be her subordinate. But Mab only begot one child with Oberon... Aurora. The youngest of all Mab's children which broke the odd cycle of thirteen, her being the fourteenth, before Oberon went missing under suspicious circumstances while leading the Wild Hunt.

If she was Oberon's only child here in Ha'real, then I didn't get what she was trying to tell me. I'd have to think on that.

Then she sighed in frustration and put a smile back on her lips, which just made me look at them as they glistened in the lights... lights? There were none visible in the space. Must be magic.

Her next question threw me for a loop.

"What do you know about DNA? Fae DNA to be precise?"

Not knowing where this was going I shrugged. "Not much, just that DNA is the code for all of us, and that any Fae trace DNA, in any case, has to be put in a stasis field or it degrades in hours even though something like a Fae's severed limb will last forever, never decaying and can even be reattached at a later date, days, years, or even centuries later."

She was looking at the door, looking rushed as she said quickly, "You should brush up on the population levels of the Leviathan over the years and why Equilibrium cannot be reached at this time."

She kept looking at the door, a frantic expression on her face but then she blinked and said, "Wait. You aren't the Knith Shade of the Beta-Stack Reproduction Clinic are you?"

I blinked at her in shock. How did she know that? Her eyes widened in what looked almost like joyful recognition.

Then I was spasming on the ground, my armor's systems shorting and my playlist started blaring in my ears, everything seemed to be spinning and I couldn't orient myself as "Bohemian Rhapsody" threatened to shatter my eardrums. Then everything went silent, and I could smell burning hair and electronics as a rich soprano voice as chilly as the heart of winter itself demanded, as I found myself held in an unyielding grip of magic which was causing ice to form on my skin, "What is that... Human, doing in my house!?"

CHAPTER 7
Another Brick In The Wall

I shook my head to clear it and focus on what was happening. And my eyes widened at Graz's body laying a couple inches in front of my face. Oh thank the gods, she was still breathing.

I felt the vice-like grip of this cold magic which held me, and I growled out as I pushed against it, "Let... go... of... me!" And the ice that was forming a cocoon around me cracked a little. It wasn't real ice, it was magic, cold magic. But I still had my scatter armor on so it couldn't get a purchase on me, so I screamed, "Get off!" at the magic, and it crackled and broke as I forced myself up to my knees, throwing my smoking helmet aside, then I stood and looked up. That was my mistake.

I already recognized the voice and knew whose icy magic that had been, but I was still disoriented and made the mistake of looking into the face of beauty incarnate, and she was my entire world as I fell back to my knees to worship at her feet. All I knew was her and my desire to please the Winter Lady, Queen Mab. My goddess.

She said in such a hypnotic tone, "You're a resilient one, how did you break that binding? What a wonderful pet you will make. Would you like that... pet?"

I was nodding frantically, I would do anything to be at her side, I would tear out my own still beating heart and hand it to her if she asked. She said, "A deal then? A trade of a kiss for your free will?"

Another voice said, "Mother don't. It's cruel."

I knew that other voice. But my goddess was going to trade a kiss for me to belong to her. I was on the cusp of an orgasm at the thought of her lips on mine as I stood on shaky legs to move up to her. She parted her lips in anticipation, like a lover. She was love, she was everything, and I was nothing.

I hesitated and shook my head. No, I wasn't nothing. I was Nobody. That was the true name I had adopted in my head, as a reminder that I was more than those who believed it. What was I doing? I blinked, seeing I was in her arms as she leaned in to kiss me with blue lips glistening with ice, and glanced over to see a terrified Aurora tugging at her mother's arm in a useless attempt to stop her.

I looked up at Mab's cheek, not making the same mistake twice, and I growled out, "Get off me, you bitch!" And I shoved her away.

Dozens of pikes were jabbed in at me, a couple penetrating armor and skin while most stopped shy of stabbing me. I grunted with the pain, which cleared my head. Mab looked amazed as she studied me. "Fascinating. She broke my thrall. No human has ever done that, even against the lesser lords. Maybe she will make a more interesting plaything than I thought, in recompense for her trespass into my palace."

She made a dismissing motion and the Captain of the guard said, "But my Queen, she laid hands upon the Winter Lady. She called you a bitch. There is but one punishment for such an act."

Mab chuckled as the guards pulled back, then with another dismissive gesture, they reluctantly left the rooms we were occupying while she said as she stepped around me, appraising me like I was a cow she was going to buy at market, "Well to be fair, I am a bitch. But I'm more interested in how she could possibly break my thrall and my binding."

Were all Fae stupid? Scatter Armor was designed to break apart magic, scatter it as it implies. I shuddered in delight at her voice as I shook off the last of the artificial blind devotion I had felt toward her. Then I shuddered in fear because I remember just how right it felt under her gaze and how I didn't even want to resist. So that was Fae glamour? It made all the Greater Fae on the ship suddenly terrifying to me.

And while under thrall I almost made a bargain with her to lose my free will that any court would uphold. A deal struck with a Fae was a binding contract. That was the danger of dealing with the tricksters.

I stooped and scooped up Graz before someone inadvertently stepped on her. I cupped her protectively to me and Aurora said, "See mother, she's not like the other Humans, she protects the Fae."

Holding up a halting hand I looked at a point in space beside the Winter Lady's face, and said while I pulled a mag-strap from my belt and saw it sparking and shorting before dropping the now useless thing to the deck and saying, "Queen Mab, I bind you by law for assaulting an Enforcer of the Brigade while on official business, questioning a person of interest in a case."

The woman chuckled, then started laughing, then doubled over she was laughing so hard. I said pointedly, "Nobody is above the law. That is how the charter was written before Exodus."

She stopped laughing immediately. "Oh. You're serious. Pet, you need to walk away before I get another ice sculpture to decorate my rooms."

"I'm nobody's pet. Now are you coming with me or do I tell the world that the Fae do not honor contracts when it is inconvenient for them? That Queen Mab does not honor her own bargains?"

Her violet eyes started chilling, and I could see the air crystallizing into a fog around them. They really were pretty eyes, just like Aurora's. She looked half affronted, half incensed and I wondered what life would be like as an ice sculpture. Probably pretty boring... and cold.

But the Queen of the Fae looked at the ceiling. "Mother, please display the Fae Exodus Treaty."

Mother responded in a decidedly cold and artificially tinny and robotic voice, "Displaying Fae Exodus Treaty. Seven point three terabytes."

Seven terabytes!? What kind of contract was it?

She sighed and said, "The law enforcement section please."

Again, the emotionless voice said, "Displaying shipboard law enforcement section three hundred and thirty thousand two hundred and three slash A. Four hundred-point seven gigabytes."

I was blinking at some of the terms as they shot past, like what color icing was allowed on cakes by vendors in the A and B-Rings during any given season onboard. Or how many square feet of roads were allowed per acre of forest in the A-Rings. To what breeds of non-fae birds were allowed free flight in the upper rings of the stacks. Then the Law Enforcement heading finally scrolled up.

Did all of these ridiculous things need to be negotiated before the Leviathan was launched?

The Queen asked, "Subsections pertaining to arrest authority of Enforcers."

"Seven relevant sections, seven hundred and ninety regulations."

She huffed. "Why can't this stupid machine anticipate what I'm asking for? This is why technology will never replace magic."

The irony of her saying that while standing in the Worldship, the most advanced piece of engineering ever created, which saved her entire race from extinction, seemed lost on her. Though I had to stop a grin when Aurora covered her smile with a hand.

Mab started reading but got frustrated and asked, "Is there any entry pertaining to Fae exemption from arrest, you talking tin can?"

The disconnected voice stated, "There is no such exemption, all citizens are subject to arrest for committing any infraction deemed illegal at the time which it is committed, or is suspect of a crime. All citizens are entitled due process and legal counsel as per section..."

"Shut up." She actually looked at a loss for words.

I prompted with a crooked smirk on my face, "Mother, what is the citizenship status of the Winter Lady?"

The tinny disaffected voice droned without emotion, "The status of the Winter Lady, AKA Queen Mab, AKA Mab of House Ashryver, AKA Mable, citizenship is – currently active, citizen number F-000001."

Huh? Whaaaa? Mable?

I dared her with my eyes. "And is she subject to arrest if she assaults a duly appointed officer of the Enforcer Brigade?"

"All citizens are subject to..."

Mab waved her hand to cut Mother off, then purred as she licked her lips, looking at me, while I looked at the wall behind her. "Oooh, this one is good. I would so love a pet like her. She's not afraid of the consequences in challenging us. We need her negotiating our contracts for us."

"Stop it, mother."

She looked at Aurora and then cocked a brow. "Oh I see, you already want her as your pet, daughter."

The Queen of the Fae told me, "Oh the pleasures you will be denied now. So what deal can we make to avoid all the unpleasantness that is sure to follow?"

She was almost purring again, and the fact that she looked like Aurora's sister more than her mother, since all Fae look to be just barely adult, had me heating up inappropriately as echos of the feeling of belonging to her rippled through me. Forever young.

Mab looked as if she could read my mind as a seductive smirk grew on her lips and she somehow seemed to move into the most enticing of feminine poses. Gods be damned. I actually growled in frustration, pushing aside the inappropriate arousal, which got her tittering then standing up straight again.

I said, "You want to make a deal? Fine, I won't bring you in, but I need full access to your daughter..." Remembering I was dealing with a Fae, I pointed at Rory, "...Aurora, during my investigation... unfettered."

Mab nodded slowly and said, "We have a deal, you do not arrest me, and you can be my daughter's lapdog until..."

I cocked an eyebrow. I knew that wording would have landed me on all fours with a wagging tail, following her daughter around.

She reworded with a smirk, "And you will have full unfettered access to Princess Aurora until your case is concluded."

Sticking my hand out to shake, she just shook her head and insisted, "Sealed with a kiss."

That was too dangerous. When a deal was sealed with a kiss, the Fae would be able to claim right of ownership over someone if they broke the bargain.

I shook my head at that and she shrugged and held her wrists out for me to take her. Rory sighed heavily. "Just do it. This is a better outcome than I would have thought."

I sighed, I wasn't going to arrest her, so my part of the bargain was done, so I said, "Fine." Then moved in to peck her cheek. She grabbed both sides of my face and kissed me full on the mouth and I gasped as cold power flowed into me and I shivered as it felt as if every cell in my body chilled. My lips were burning and some residual of her earlier whammy on me had me kissing back for a moment before she pulled away, and my body warmed again except my lips.

She hissed in my ear, a warning whisper, as I felt my lips still burning with the cold, "Know this, as punishment for even threatening to tell others I do not honor my deals, you're now marked by me. You spread even a rumor insinuating that, and the mark will activate and you will be the next ice maiden to adorn my bedchambers, forever frozen in ice to watch as I take my endless stream of lovers in bed in front of you. Do we understand each other, Enforcer?"

I swallowed as a primal fear urged me to run far and fast and I just nodded dumbly. She smiled sweetly at that and then I was seeing stars as she slapped me harder than I've ever been hit in my life.

I growled out as I held my stinging cheek, "Son of a bitch!" Then I glared at her and said, "Why did you assault me again when you were free and clear? Now I'm going to have to..."

"You should really pay attention to the wording of any deals with the Fae, child. We did not specify what you would not arrest me for, just that you promised not to arrest me. That was for daring to lay hands on me. And as smart as you think you are, making a mockery of me in my own house, you'll always remember the fact that you had been broken, and bowed to me and willingly wanted to be owned by me, even if it was for just a moment before the thrall was snapped."

"Mom, now you really are being a bitch."

A moment later in an explosion of burning ice bits, a little pup with violet eyes was sitting where Aurora had been. Her mother said, "Bitch, am I? You can be a bitch for a few hours and see if that doesn't quell this rebellious streak." The puppy looked down at her big floppy paws and whined. Mab picked her up and said in baby talk, "There, there, mommy still loves you. You just need to choose your words more carefully."

Oh just great, the murder suspect I needed to question, just got turned into a dog for defending me against her terrifying mother. Then the Winter Lady reached out and I flinched, but she just placed a hand on my cheek almost lovingly and said ever so sweetly, "As much as you amuse me, I would suggest you leave now before I come up with something else to do with you, child."

I nodded in earnest as she added, "You do intrigue me, Enforcer. No one has ever broken my thrall, and that makes you... interesting."

Oh, gods. I didn't want to be interesting to Mab. I exhaled, and my breath fogged up as it passed my still cold feeling lips, making me think of her threat. Knith and ice sculpture? No mixie.

I just left my helmet and other shorted equipment on the floor and I ran, cradling a still unconscious Graz. J'real and Nyx looked concerned for me as I ran past. As I exited into the labyrinth of corridors, I found I was instead stumbling down the stairs outside of the main palace doors.

I didn't want to think about that. Just then I wanted to go, to run and to hide.

The transport was there, the guards around it. Captain Delphine's eyes flicked to my mouth then she smirked and opened her mouth to say something, but I got right in her face, "One word... just one word and I'm hauling your ass in. My deal with Mab didn't include your indiscretion. So laugh it up Fae girl!"

To my surprise, she shut it. I added as I slipped into the vessel, "I'll be back when your Princess isn't such a bitch. It was part of the deal so don't even think of harassing me."

I told the craft, "Spoke terminal." I tore off a section of fried scatter armor and tore the skin suit to get at the two wounds I received from the guards who didn't have as good of control over their pikes as the others... or did they?

The bleeding wounds were shallow. I pulled the med kit from the vessel's wall and pulled out the sterilizer and two synth-skin patches. I just needed to stop the bleeding, I was an incredibly fast healer for a human. I sprayed the wounds liberally, washing away the blood, and the clotting agent went to work immediately. Then I slapped on the synth-skin patches and activated them. The low level magic cooked off in them as they bonded with my surface skin.

They would flake off in the next twelve hours or so. I could hit

Med-Tech at Central to have them use a dermal repair unit to heal me up in minutes, but that always itched, my natural healing would have me good as new in a day or two, minus the itching.

Once I was satisfied I wasn't in danger of bleeding out, then I started frantically examining Graz.

She peeked up at me, opening one eye, then sat up. "Damn Knith, did you really face down Queen Mab? I take it back, you don't have big balls, you got some huge boulders, lady."

I blinked and asked in incredulity, "Graz! You're ok? Wait, you were faking it? How much did you see?"

She shrugged. "Pretty much everything. Including your little makeout session with the Winter Lady. I was only out for a second when all that power hit you I was blown off your shoulder."

I shoved her shoulder with a finger. "I was scared to death for you and you were faking it!?"

She shrugged. "You don't want the Winter Lady to notice you when she is in a bad mood and a stupid Human null is making her look bad."

As I sat at a loss for words, she pointed at me. "Umm... Knith? Your lips are blue."

I reached up to touch them and they clinked when my fried gauntlet fingers touched them. What the hells? She said, "They look like glass."

I exhaled in panic, my breath fogging again as I whispered, "Or ice?"

There was nothing for it now. Just then I wanted to get back down-ring and get new gear and try to solve this damned case so I'd never had to deal with the Greater Fae again. I went to hit my wrist coms but saw a melted piece of slag where it should have been.

I asked the transport, "Mother?"

There was no answer. Of course, it seemed the Fae were allergic to technology so why would they put a simple uplink in their vessels?

Graz offered a tiny wrist console to me and I sighed and took it and held it against my ear canal and asked, "Mother?"

She was there, voice filled with emotion, "Knith. I was so afraid for you." I sighed with a smile, then I realized why she didn't sound like her in the palace. She didn't want the Fae to know how... alive she was. I know what happens to things the Fae find intriguing. So she was playing dumb with them. Has she always done that over the centuries with them?

I closed my eyes as we flew and asked, "Can you just play me some music, I think I've got more of an education with dealing with Fae than I ever wanted."

In a small voice, she chirped, "Ok."

I sighed and let a song called "Another Brick In The Wall" take me away until we reached the spoke.

CHAPTER 8
Rebel Yell

Once I got back to my Tac-Bike, I sighed in relief, breath fogging between my lips. Then I blurted out a squeak of nervous laughter when Graz randomly asked, "So, is she a good kisser?" I think I needed that, I had been on the verge of a breakdown ever since we left Mab's presence, and I'm pretty sure the little Sprite knew that. And I appreciated the distraction.

She smirked. "No, really. Like was it..."

I zipped her lips and she just grinned at me, knowing her attempt to get me out of my mind space had worked.

As we glided through light traffic toward the barracks, I thought hard about what I had learned. Not much at all besides the murder weapon belonging to Rory and she didn't seem concerned about it. I didn't get my questions answered and walked away with even more.

I was sure Aurora was trying to tell me something but she either couldn't or was physically unable to talk about it.

I laid it out so I could try to see the larger picture. One, why had she asked me about Fae DNA? Two, why had she asked about population levels and Equilibrium? They had been the same since Exodus, that is why I was actually born in the damn Clinic. If birth levels slip for any race, then children are gestated in a lab to keep the population at Equilibrium. And Three, I have never been so terrified in my life because Mab was right.

I kept dwelling on how easily she had broken me with just a glance at her face. I was truly about to give her my free will happily because, at that moment, I hadn't even mattered because Mab had been my everything.... and I hated her for it. I have never hated anyone in my life, and I could see it for the poison it was, which just made me hate her even more for making me feel this way. Was I damaged? Compromised now?

Hmmm... Four, what had she tried to tell me about Oberon's children? And how was any of this connected to the murders? Looks like I had my work cut out for me.

As I pulled up to Control, half the Day Lights in the ring powered down. What the hells? A malfunction of that magnitude hasn't happened in generations. I pitied the poor engineers and techs who were going to have to troubleshoot that.

Graz buzzed away toward the roof as I headed up the steps to the main door. Ah, is that how they got into my quarters? The building vents? I assumed she was going to check on her family.

I refocused on the case as I reached the doors. So, each of the victims had organs that allowed them to store or absorb magic. And they were taken. Wait... she had said, "There is just one anomaly." Did the murderer slip up?

Then I remembered that the Woodling's horns were taken, they weren't an organ. Was that significant?

I headed straight to the locker room for a shower and to get new gear before I pursued anything. Some of the Enforcers I passed were looking at me funny, and a couple of them actually turned and scurried off like they didn't want to be near me. What was that all about?

A minute later I was cursing under a freezing cold shower. "Son of a..." I tapped the hot icon repeatedly, but the temperature stayed the same. Were the hot water processors out now too? The addition of the cold water made my breath fog even more, reminding me of what Mab had done to me. I leaned in to look in the small mirror on the wall behind the shower controls that the men used to shave.

I blinked, Graz was right, my lips looked to be semi-translucent blue-tinted ice. The water droplets that had landed on them froze in place. I reached up and wiped the little frozen beads off, and it was like my fingers slid over slick glass, but I could feel my touch like my lips were still skin. Icy cold skin.

What had Mab done to me?

I exhaled and went about finishing the shower before I froze to death then just as I was reaching for a towel from the cart by the door, Captain Yon stepped in and glared at me. "Shade, Commander Reise's Office. Now."

I blinked at him and asked sarcastically, "Can I get dressed first?"

The Centaur stared at me impassively for a moment, then turned and trotted off, calling back, "Be there in ten. Do not keep the old man waiting."

Now what? This was not shaping up to be my day.

I glanced over to the couple men and women showering as they whispered to each other as they rushed through the cold showers. Ok, something was definitely going on that I was not privy to.

After dressing in a fresh set of sensor contact garments I headed to supply, just outside of the locker rooms and dropped the bag of shorted equipment and fried armor. I didn't have my helmet anymore as I had tossed the burning and sparking thing on the floor of Rory's lab.

Enforcer Clemmens looked up at me. One of the few humans on staff who was respected by everyone, mostly because he was what stood between you and quality, next-gen gear and old recycled crap that always had a funky smell to it, from the sweat of the many people who wore it before you, and sterilization fluids. No amount of photon or sonic baths could get the smell totally out.

The irises of his eye implants sparkled as I'm sure he was trying to read the status and identification data from the slag. He reached out and shook his head then reached out with the ancillary arms he had grafted to his augmented spinal cluster. While he crossed his one biological arm and flesh-like left cybernetic arm over his chest.

"If I isn't Miss Destructo. Damn it Shade, this is the second set of SA's this year. You don't have to put yourself in danger every second to keep up with the Paras. You're gonna get yourself messed up worse than you mess up my equipment one of these days."

He picked up a trash bin, and instead of sifting through the remains of my Scatter Armor for anything salvageable, he just slid it all in. "If you insist on taking so many chances, you could at least get augments. The new cybernetic implants are amazing, direct neural link." He flexed the fingers on his new left arm. "Zero response lag and ninety-eight percent touch receptors, body temperature magi-tech circuitry. You can't even tell it's cyber. It's how I did fifteen tours in the Brigade and kept up with all the other races before they sat my ass down here on gear duty for daring to get old."

I smiled at the man. He was always trying to get me to get augments. But I kept up just fine being unmodded. Rough on equipment and myself, sure, but my arrest and case closure records were on par or above my more physically, and magically inclined contemporaries.

Sighing I said, "Sorry Zak, it just sort of shorted on me. I need a new set of SA's... and wrist console... and standard Tac gear... oh and my MMGs are toast too. I'm sort of in a hurry, brass wants me like five minutes ago."

His sigh eclipsed mine as he turned back to his shelves and must have sent the code with a thought, to have the bins start cycling through on the railed shelves. He stopped on some ancient-looking armor that didn't even have scatter plates. Scratches and even some oxidation buildup at some cracks. Oh lord, not even hard contact points for a skin suit, it would be rubbing through the skinsuit and my skin in no time.

The smile he shot me was positively evil. "Oh come on, Zak...

don't do that to me."

He smirked, rolled his eyes and then grabbed the bin beside it, with new SAs in vacuum-sealed bags, and armament, and Tac gear. I told him, "I love you, man."

He snorted and then grabbed a helmet in a box on his desk and sighed heavily, hesitated, then handed it to me. "Newest experimental model straight from R&D. Predictive and adaptive circuitry with surface thought synaptic scanning. Direct multiphasic link to Mother, giving her access to your auditory and optic nerves. And some stuff you can't use since you don't even have a com jack, you Luddite."

He held onto it when I tried to take it. An ancillary arm shook a finger at me. "I'd be giving you the shit armor and telling you to suck vacuum if you complained, and if I didn't need a lab rat. You need to log your experiences for all the systems on a daily basis. That is if you're still an Enforcer after the Commander and President are done with you."

What? The President? What does she want with me?

He chuckled at my confusion. "You really don't know what a shit-pile you just kicked, do you? Keep frosty or I'm sure you'll be begging to go suck hard vacuum."

Well, fuck me sideways. I knew the fallout was probably going to be bad, but I'm only going where the evidence takes me. I sat at the bench outside supply after I synced the new gear with my retina and DNA lockout codes with Zak. Then I geared up.

I almost shuddered as the new skinsuit adapted to my shape, burning off the molding spell infused in the fibers. After having every nerve in my body shorted out by Mab's magic, my skin was more sensitive now, like it was recovering from frost burns. Then I slapped on the SA, and they reconfigured to my form but I didn't feel any spells cooking off.

I looked up to see Zak watching smugly. "That's Mark-6 gear, all reconfigurable nano-panels instead of the magi-tech fitting." I nodded in appreciation, that meant if I gained or lost mass, I wouldn't have to bring it in to have it re-fitted.

After I put the helmet on, and the moment it registered me, by imprinting to my DNA scan and mating with my armor, I was panicking as the visor shut and polarized without me telling it. And systems powered up and down at random, and I saw flashes of light in my head and snaps and crackles of sound being amplified, then cut off in privacy mode, leaving me reeling.

I took a deep breath and realized I couldn't, the re-breathers were locked down.

I was deaf, blind, and gasping. Shit, I needed to breathe. And the re-breathers started cycling air to me as I inhaled deeply at that thought. Then the visor depolarized and I could see again. I gave blink commands and nothing. I just wanted the damn visor to raise and it did with a snick. Then I got it. He did say surface synaptic scanning, so just think it... and... Mother said, "Hello Knith." But not through the helmet, nor the earbuds which I realized this helmet didn't have.

I whispered as Zak chuckled, "Mother? Are you in my head?"

She chirped out in a happy tone, "I have direct access to your auditory and optical nerves. I can see and hear what you do and can feed you audio or..." The clearest heads up display bloomed around me in my head-space and the peripherals readjusted as my eyes focused on different things.

This was incredible. Then I freaked the hells out when Mother said, "Thank you."

I thought "You can hear my thoughts?"

"I'm interfacing with the neural net scanning from the helmet and can... sort of. Just the surface thoughts if you are intent on something." Did I really want an AI poking around inside my mind? I trusted Mother but resolved to keep my thoughts to myself as much as possible so I could pretend I had some privacy.

I stood finally and packed my Tac gear in the belt pouches, then took the harmonica from my shoulder bag, examined it for any damage from Mab's magic, but it was surprisingly in pristine condition, so I slipped it into a pouch on my waist. I don't know why. I think I just liked the nostalgia and the fact that it was possibly as old as the Leviathan herself.

"Hey, I'm not old, I'm..."

I muttered, "Mother, can you just pretend to not poke around in my thoughts?"

"You're loud. You need to learn to keep your thoughts deep."

I sighed, I'd never win.

"Good girl."

"Go space yourself, Mother."

She actually giggled?

I stood and told Zak as I handed him all the vacuum bags to be recycled, "Thanks for this. I'm not sure about this gods be damned helmet though. I'll catch you later." I lifted a hand as I walked past his window, and he held out his four hands and I high fived them all.

He called after me as I marched to my probable doom. "Do I get your things if they space you, Shade?"

I just flipped him off as I walked toward the lifts.

Then when the doors closed, after the three occupants saw me step on and they all but ran out of the car, I took a moment to run a gauntlet along the armor. It fit better than a glove and seemed to move with me organically, were the nano-panels reconfiguring with the flexing of my muscles? This was nice.

We shot up to the upper level and I hesitated. I looked out the clear outer wall of the lift car to see the yellow air quality and circulation lights flashing along the bulkhead for the interior corridors. I added that to all the other things not working and I felt the blood draining from my face. Mother Fairy humper, this was punishment by the Fae, wasn't it?

To keep my mind off of all the repercussions of the Fae restrictions on all the amenities that make life comfortable on the world, and knowing I was likely the most hated human on board just then, I tried to concentrate on the case.

Something simple... the Woodling horns. Why would the killer take those if they were after the magical organs of those rare races? Did they have some significance or some value?

"Woodling horns are a potent aphrodisiac for the greater Fae. Woodlings sell horn shavings to the Fae Lords and Ladies for ten thousand chit tokens an ounce. And adult horns weigh an average of three pounds each which they shed once every hundred and fifty years."

I squeaked in surprise, "Mother! Out of my head." Then I asked right after, "An aphrodisiac for greater Fae? What about for other races?"

"It has no effect on other races except through a Fae who ingests it, who can share the experience of it through their magic with anyone they have sexual relations with."

Ah... so basically if they want to whore around and have others share the heightened experience. I chuckled. "If it didn't just work for Fae, it would be in high demand at the adult sections of the supply and provision shops. Or at the brothels on the world..." I trailed off as I added in a whisper as my gut told me, "Or off the world like a certain Fae Lord that Mac had told us about."

Did he know something? I thought it odd for him to bring it up when he did. I felt as if everyone, in this case knew things I didn't, and were trying to give me clues instead of speaking plainly.

"Mother?"

"In contact with the Underhill Brothel to see when he is next available. I just booked you an hour with him tonight, at eight PM."

I smiled, she's always been on the same page with me whenever I was brainstorming. I felt like she had my back.

She chirped, "Always."

I sighed at the thought butinski, then stiffened as the lift finally slowed and stopped. I took a deep breath and stepped out into the waiting lobby for the Commander's office and froze. By the gods! Commander Reise was standing by his personal assistant's desk, having a heated discussion with President Yang! Her half-elven features making her look elegant, even with the searing look she was directing toward me.

They were surrounded by the Presidential Security Unit in their heavy armor and heavily modded cybernetic bodies. Then everyone stopped and turned to look at me, and I felt suddenly two inches tall.

That's how I found myself demoted down two ranks and pay grades, down here in virtual zero-G in the guard booth at the mines of the Heart just two hours later. The three other human Enforcers in the pressurized booth wore exoskeletons, telling me they have been down here a very very long time. And the odds of me ever getting out of here and back patrolling a beat up-ring were negligible.

I've never been dressed down by a President before. And boy could she yell, and cuss, in six languages, only four of which I understood. And the damn gorgeous middle-aged halfling looked fabulous while making me feel like the worst human being who was ever born for questioning a Fae Princess in a murder investigation.

It seems eight systems, two critical had started malfunctioning the moment I left the A-Ring, and all but two magically started working again the moment I was sent down here to my own personal hell. The Fae apologize for any inconvenience the unfortunate malfunctions have caused, and should have hot water and Day Lights restored in a week.

But... I was positive I did the right thing. We shouldn't give the Fae a free pass just because they hold the literal power on the world. I was feeling defiant as I thought, "Mother?" She anticipated that and my playlist started pounding in my ears, filling my head like I was sitting in a concert hall for the performance of "Rebel Yell" by a man named Billy Idol.

I smirked and pulled up a downlink from the core to check out the other questions that were raised from my ill-fated visit to Ha'real. As I watched the vac-suited prisoners through the windows, heading into the unpressurized mines for ore processing, I twitched my fingers slightly on the virtual keypad to pull up population and Equilibrium records which I had thought I knew all about. I mean everyone did and it was all common sense.

How wrong I was.

CHAPTER 9
Wake Me Up Inside

What I found out would have had my jaw on the floor if I wasn't in virtual zero G in the microgravity down here. Hells, I needed the mag-circuits in my boots powered just to keep my feet on the floor. Every child is taught the history of the Leviathan. And about population Equilibrium. The Worldship can only sustain a specific number of souls, with an acceptable safety margin, or the whole delicate ecosystem on the world could be thrown out of balance.

So by the charter, population levels for all races are to be kept at the same levels as they were upon Exodus. Which, is why I exist. During a period of low Human or other race's birthrates, the Reproduction Clinic will either gestate or clone babies to replenish numbers. It is why the Clinic exists.

And the fluctuations in populations has remained static since launch, with acceptable fluctuations within a tenth of a percent over time. The most noticeable was the Human population that seems to be in chaotic flux all the time, as we are such a short-lived species. For every thousand humans who die, every year, only three or four citizens of other races die.

Every few years, we lose some lesser Fae who die in accidents or something similar. There was even a lesser Fae illness that swept through the stacks seven centuries ago that actually killed off a

significant number of lesser Fae including Sprites and Pixies. But
their numbers are almost back to Equilibrium now.

I had to smile at that, Graz's children were the latest Sprites
born, and that brings their numbers up to just shy of launch day
numbers.

And I figured that is was just common sense that the Greater Fae
were eternal, so their numbers were unchanging. But I was shocked
to find that since Exodus, the Leviathan has actually lost twenty-five
Greater Fae over the eons of her journey. It seems they are not
immune to freak accidents either... and even one murder in the early
years.

And two are marked as inactive. After some digging it seems
they are still alive, just as ice sculptures, engaged in the act of coitus,
adorning the Winter Lady's bedchambers. One had been a lover
who was dallying around with one of the palace staff behind Mab's
back. She... 'sentenced' them to that fate, to be frozen on the cusp of
release just as she had found them the day she walked in on them,
until the day of Land Fall, when the Fae walk on the Ground again.
She was truly wicked.

I shivered, my breath fogging on my lips as I decided I had
gotten off easy. Maybe I should send her a fruit basket or something
for sparing me. Or would that be too close to a thank you?

The more striking information is that no Fae children had ever
been born to take the place of the ones lost, and maintain the
Equilibrium. Though many mating and breeding attempts were

made, it was determined that the Greater Fae were incapable of producing new progeny. The deeper I dug, the more shocking it became.

A researcher in Ha'real, a certain Winter Maiden I am acquainted with, Princess Aurora, had determined that it was tied to the nature of the Fae. They, though they looked and felt and lived and laughed like any other living beings, were actually magic incarnate. Their very cells, down to the DNA were constructed of magic made physical.

This is why she had asked me what I knew of their DNA. And it seems that their power came from the very Earth itself. But now, on the ship, the only pieces of Earth that remain is the soil and stone on the upper rings, and the artifacts of immense power the Fae used to run the ship.

Since there is so little actual 'Earth' and most of the power of the artifacts are used to keep us all alive, there isn't enough new magic available for two Fae to conceive a child. And they didn't know if the problem would solve itself when we reached our new home, and the new planet would share its magic with the Fae.

Two teams, one from the Unseelie Winter Court and one from the Seelie Summer Court have been researching a means to restore Equilibrium, to allow for new Greater Fae to be born.

Aurora has led the Unseelie Court team and has had many spectacular failures over the centuries, nothing promising except almost fifty years ago, she had some sort experiment going on at the

Beta-Stack Reproduction Clinic with human embryos.

I swallowed as I typed out a query. And Mother asked instead in a small voice, "Are you sure you want that information?"

I exhaled in a huff, causing my fellow Enforcers to turn to me. "What, Freshie? The boredom at this posting beneath you? Should have thought of that before you committed career suicide with the Fae Bitch Queen."

My lips pulsed, and I felt more of my skin icing. I silently pleaded with whatever spell it was that I hadn't said it... well I thought it but didn't say it. Doh! The ice spread a little more. Ok, think happy thoughts. I said hoarsely, "You best not let Mab hearing you say that. And my name is Shade, not Freshie, Harris."

He shook his head and Andrews told me in a voice full of exhaustion, "Names don't matter, we're all nobodies down here. The sooner you learn that the sooner you'll accept that you'll never get another posting. Take my advice and just quit the Brigade now or you'll end up a lifer down here like us. Needing an exo-suit just to walk up-ring."

I was never going to quit, the Brigade was my life, where I could make a difference. I looked out the window to the constant stream of prisoners moving ore. A lot of difference I could make here. I sighed then smirked as I said, "You're right Andrews, I'm Nobody."

With a silent plea, Mother had more of that anthropological music playing inside my head, "Wake Me Up Inside" by a group called Evanescence, as I continued my covert research. I was quickly becoming addicted to this new helmet's interface. It was like nothing I had seen before. Those geeks in R&D were going to be getting a fruit basket from me too.

I tried to think a scolding look, and that got Mother to unlock the information I wanted... no, needed to see. And there was my name... the only name listed in a failed test group of one hundred test inseminations in one of Rory's tests. I wound up being the only embryo to be produced, and after I didn't show the expected results, she had moved her research on to attempts to clone Fae DNA structures as biological instead of magical for the past forty-plus years.

So... I was what? Some sort of failed attempt to breed a new Fae child? I was a failed experiment? Well, the joke is on them, I'm one hundred percent, red-blooded human. Congratulations Winter Maiden, you made a null.

I don't know why I was so angry and frustrated just then. I was what I was. Now her recognizing my name made sense.

I punched the panel in front of me and the transparent ceramic surface cracked in a spiderweb pattern. The others looked at me and I grinned sheepishly, "Sorry, muscle spasm. Wow, this panel looks defective, maintenance should really do something about it."

They actually just turned away to stare out the window, Andrews muttered, "Welcome to Hell, Shade."

A flashing in my peripheral had me looking at the other team's attempts. The Seelie Court's experiments were all about combining tissues and genes from other species to create a vessel compatible with Fae physiology. That if they could build a biological shell that could hold Fae energy, then they could just use a glamour, or even a much more difficult physical transformation into a more pleasing Fae form.

I thought about that and looked something up. It seemed that very few Greater Fae had the power to successfully change the physical structure of a living being into something else. Which made Mab twice as scary to me now because she had pupped her daughter with just a thought, no casting involved.

The Summer Lady disbanded the attempts recently as they had had eons of failures even though the man running the attempts, a lesser Fae Lord, Sindri... hmm... no house was listed for him, had insisted he could do it and beat Rory to the solution to repopulate the Fae race on the world.

I hesitated then rewound with my eyes and looked at the date of the disbandment of his team, and the date of the first killing. Two weeks apart. This was something, I could feel it... but how would he have gotten a hold of that surgical scalpel from Rory's lab? A co-conspirator? That seemed unlikely as absolutely terrifying as Mab was. Imagine if she had found some sort of mole in her palace, what she would do to them if she found them.

And Rory had said that only her, her mother, her guards, and the children of Oberon had access. And everyone knew that Princess Aurora was the only child Mab and Oberon had. So that pointed back at Rory again.

Why did I not want it to be her so badly? Well besides the fact I found her funny, intelligent, and by the gods was she sexy... ok, fine, I was attracted to a probable serial killer. It fit in with the day I was having so why not?

Something was niggling at the back of my mind then I realized what. I typed to Mother. "Is there a list of the children Oberon had with the Summer Lady and others before he married Mab to be her second?"

A list of thirteen names appeared. What was it with Fae and having thirteen children? I looked at the familiar names, the princesses and princes of Summer.

Fae were people too. I remember some talk of the disappearance of Oberon while he was out leading the Wild Hunt, there was some whisperings in the Fae courts about infidelity. I had assumed it was Mab straying, she is famous for her bedroom dalliances. It is something in her Fae nature to conquer those she sees as a threat, she was a very sexual creature, and she used her considerable gifts to do so.

Something clicked in me. Was that why she took delight in reminding me that she had broken my will in but a glance and longing for her? Reminding me who was Queen and I could never measure up? The bitch! My cheeks chilled as the ice spread. Oh, space me! I wasn't thinking about telling anyone she went back on her word, that's what the curse was for, not just thinking ill of her.

I sighed and had Mother show me the internal helmet cam view. Half of my lower jaw was now translucent blue ice, from my lower lip down. I flexed my mouth and lips and it acted just like normal skin, but I could see the moisture in the air frosting as it condensed around it. Fuck me sideways and space me naked.

Mother offered helpfully, "It's not so bad. I think it's pretty."

I typed aggressively at her. "Yeah, it'll look pretty when I'm a gods be damned ice sculpture. I need to find a way to get her to remove this."

I sighed when the red lights started flashing inside the booth and out in the mines. The day was over. We watched as each prisoner stepped in front of us, was scanned then headed into the dormitory below the booth. Once all were accounted for, we hit the lock-down, then signed things over to the night shift and I was free to go.

I'd have to get home and change if I were going to go meet up with the dallying Fae Lord at the Underhill brothel. I didn't want to scare him off with my uniform.

Mother asked breathlessly in my ear, "A dress?"

I muttered as I pulled myself along the corridors by the grip bars, almost weightless, to the transport tubes in the trunk, "Stop eavesdropping on my mind. I half love this new helmet and half hate it."

"Stop whining... here, listen to some music, it makes you less testy."

I had to grin. She was pretty funny sometimes. Can machines

be funny?

"I'm funny. Now shush."

CHAPTER 10
When Doves Cry

A long thirty minutes later, I was up-ring and sighing in relief with my familiar weight on my feet. I was still getting the cold shoulder from everyone since Mab was still punishing the ring for my 'transgressions'. That Fae was certifiable.

Damn it!

I felt ice crackle across my lower jaw, and before I could ask, Mother showed me the interior helmet video feed. My entire lower jaw was now that weird living, flexible ice. The lights around me shone through it, causing it to glow in that bluish tint.

It went from the corners of my lips, across my jaw in a straight line and it looked more like some sort of gaudy augment than a curse which was punishing me every time I thought ill of its caster. Were spells alive?

At this rate, by the end of the week, I was going to wind up an ice chandelier or something hanging in her audience chamber, or worse, her bedchambers. I ran my tongue along my lower teeth to see if they had sensation still, and my tongue clinked against them. Son of a... my tongue was ice too. Would that affect my sense of taste? Could I eat normally, or did I have to avoid hot beverages?

I needed to speak with Rory, or maybe one of the magic defense instructors at the academy. Now this, this right here is why most humans feared magical races. I loved the diversity of the Leviathan, and embrace magic, hells, I'd love to be able to cast. But as a human, unless I was gifted in it, the best I could hope to do is some witchcraft. But that ate away at the bodies of the few witches on board. There is a reason all the stories speak of them as withered and arthritic elders.

And even the Fae don't know why there are no male witches, but they postulate that it is because human male chromosomes are defective, one leg missing from one of the natural XX chromosome pairs. It is like they see us 'lesser races' as all the same, and don't understand that it is that Y chromosome that makes them male in most cases. Though even then, that doesn't solely define their gender.

Now after my dealings with the Winter Lady, I'm starting to question whether my free acceptance of magic as just any other tool was possibly naive. Lots of my gear was magi-tech, a seamless blending of magic and technology.

In our everyday lives, we use magic items, like the synth-skin patches I had used earlier. It is so ingrained in our society that maybe I saw magic as innocuous, always there like background noise. But now that it was physically doing something to my body and I had no way of stopping it... magic was starting to make me nervous.

I exhaled as I got off the lift, my breath fogging as I did. Mother tried to cheer me up as she offered a pathetic, "Well, if it's any consolation, at least it looks pretty?"

I snorted. Ok, it was working. We stepped into my quarters and I froze. It was Sprite-ageddon. Sprites zipping all over, squealing and yelling, having what looked to be a mini pillow fight or something with daring aerial displays, dust sifting all over the floor.

Someone let out a two-tone high pitched whistle and they all turned in mid-flight and zipped down into a hole that was cut in the door of my nightstand. I sighed as I took off my helmet and slapped my forehead, dragging my hand down my face as a far too innocent looking Graz sat almost demurely on the edge of the nightstand, looking quite feminine at the time. "Uhh... hi Knith. We were just cleaning up the place... it sort of degraded into ummm..."

I cocked an eyebrow and offered, "War?"

"Yeah, that!"

I looked around, and the place did look tidy, except for the fact everything was coated in Sprite dust. "Welcome home. Uh... you look very manly. Did you do something different with your jaw?"

"Nice try, lady. I don't get distracted that easily. And I'm female, I told you that."

She chirped out quickly, "All you nulls look the same to me. So um, you look very female-ly? Womanly? Oh! Pretty!" She gave me a smile that was way into the cheesy zone with two enthusiastic thumbs up.

"Stop trying to suck up to me, buttercup. I've got too much shit falling all over me right now to worry about evicting your tiny ass."

She stood and looked back behind her. "What is it with you and your fixation with my butt? I mean, it is pretty awesome, but I mean, really, I'm a mated pollinator, go look at other people's butts. And are you calling me small?" She had her blade out at the last question.

I sighed. I didn't have time for this. "It's a figure of speech, genius. I've got to get ready now, I've someplace to be." Then I hesitated, not knowing what they had in my nightstand. "Do you and your family need anything to eat? You've been busy squatting in my quarters all day."

"On it, we've been using the hells out of your pantry. You should really lock it better. Did you know they made sugared cereal? You Bigs get all the good stuff." Ah... that would explain the hyperness in her voice. Was her whole family on a sugar high?

I moved behind my changing screen and started stripping out of my SAs and paused with my skinsuit. I could use the extra protection if I was going off-world again, but it screamed Enforcer. So I stripped out of it and almost jumped when Graz chirped from where she was sitting on top of the screen, idly kicking her feet, "So where ya going?"

I turned away and pointed away. "Hey, I'm naked here."

"Oh relax, you don't have anything my Mitzy doesn't have, or most of me either. How can you go through life without wings? You got plenty of room there on your back, miles of skin."

I pointed away again, with narrowed eyes and she buzzed off. Then I said as I went through my wardrobe, realizing that I had all of two sets of civilian clothes, or civvies, and a single dress that I had to have for special occasions. Did I really not have a personal life? I lived, ate, and breathed the Brigade.

I guess that would explain my lack of dating life too. I mean, I dated... what... ok so I've only dated three women in the past decade... or two. Well two women, a heavily modded Human with a cybercat fetish, and a Satyr, but I'm not sure if Forest Walkers had a gender. Some Humans called them Ents, but I just thought Fern was gorgeous, with all that soft moss, blooming flowers, and bewitching smile.

I thought her large wide eyes looked feminine so I called her she. And what she could do to the aching muscles of my back with her feathery soft, vinelike appendages was heaven. But winter came to the B-Ring and we sort of lost touch after she had to go and literally plant herself for three months in the soil of the parks up-ring. Ok, maybe I was so attracted to her because she never spoke, no Walkers ever did... she was the best listener ever.

I looked at the dress, it was too formal to be going to some sex den on the Remnants. So I put on some pants, a plain white blouse, my mag boots, and then on a whim to cut the goody two shoes look, I pulled out the flight jacket my first girlfriend gave me when she joined the Ready Squadron. The ace fliers who were always on point, flying in front of the Leviathan, and clearing a path through any asteroid, meteor or comet debris which crossed our path. Blowing anything larger than a Hel Ball into smaller pieces that couldn't penetrate the armor of the Skin.

Perfect, its downy lined collar could flip up to hide my jaw. I looked at my Brigade issued wrist console and sighed. I said to the air, "Looks like I'm flying solo on this one Mother. You can watch me through the world until I get into the Remnants." I still rested my belt packs crookedly on my hips though.

"Is that wise? You're already still investigating a case that you were explicitly told you were to have nothing to do with. Should you be going in without backup or me to document it?"

I stopped, and looked expectantly at one of the dozen vid ports in the room, she sighed far too convincingly before she asked, "Fuck 'em if they can't take a joke?"

I tapped the side of my nose and said, "Ding ding ding."

She grumped out, "Then at least take Myra's goggles too, they have full tech packs like your old helmet."

Ok, that would complete the Irontown Grunge look. "Good idea." Now I could take Mother with me onto the Underhill. I pulled the goggles out of a box at the bottom of the closet and looked at them. They still had half a charge. It would be a couple of decades before the fusion packs needed to be swapped out.

I smiled at them, they were stylized to look like old goggles from the beginnings of the age of flight. A turning point in human history and one of the few points in time that the "human plague" had worried the Fae. It was hard to believe that the tech inside had been so advanced a couple of decades ago that it still rivaled most of the Brigade tech today. Ready Squadron needed the best or we would be one long line of wreckage floating past Eridani Prime in a few thousand years.

I slid the goggles on with their faux leather strap and slid them to the top of my head, then tied my hair into a tight ponytail.

I turned to the changing screen and Mother was kind enough to mirrorize the surface. I looked like an extra from one of those space horror waves on the holo-consoles. I smirked, flipped the collar up, looked down a little, and could barely catch a glimpse of my jaw.

When I stepped out into the room, Graz nodded, eyes wide. "Badass."

Hey, that was almost a compliment. I hid my smile and said, "Just have a few minutes to eat before I have to get going."

"Oh yeah, that. Where did you say you were going again?"

My cheeks heated slightly as I said, "Following a lead."

Mother, always so helpful... not... supplied, "I have booked her with a Fae Lord in the brothel at Underhill tonight."

Graz's vice was an octave higher as she teased, "Oh, so making time with the Queen of the Fae gave you a taste for the denizen of Faerie, did it? No judgments here. I mean, those lords and ladies of the upper court even do it for Sprites. I mean..."

"Shut it!"

Then I inhaled long and hard and almost started coughing as my lungs were chilled. Ok, note to self, don't do that with an ice jaw. "I'm going to question him. He's a person of interest."

"Yeah, interest between the sheets!"

"Graz!" I made a zipping motion over her lips when she landed on my shoulder wiggling her brows suggestively. I explained, "It seems Woodling horn is a potent aphrodisiac for the greater Fae. I figured, that if there was a Fae Lord slumming it down in a brothel off-world, maybe he had a little help." I mimed snorting drugs.

The Sprite blinked then smiled. "Hey, that's actually pretty smart." Then she added, "Did Mother think of it?"

I flicked her with a finger, sending her buzzing off giggling like a mad pollinator, and then she zipped into the nightstand calling out, "Don't do anything I wouldn't do." More muffled giggling ensued.

After a quick meal, nothing heated, I headed out. The lights of the stars and nebula light the sky and the dim navigation lights lit the roads and buildings. I grabbed the lone cab on the streets that was heading toward the clubbing and drinking districts. I really wasn't in the mood for a Jump pod. And with my new financial situation, I wouldn't be able to splurge like this again anytime soon.

When I gave my destination, the cabbie gave me a knowing smile on his goat face. I let him think whatever he wanted. "Five extra chits if you can get me there in fifteen." The extra Gs of his acceleration had me smirking as I was pushed back into my seat. He did it in fourteen. Though there was a harrowing moment in the spoke heading down to D-Ring, when he used radial acceleration to ride the walls to drive above the light traffic.

I thumbed his payment pad and typed in an extra ten chits, he was worth it. I double blinked and mother took a picture of his ID with the goggles. If I needed to be somewhere yesterday, I was sure to request him. Then I was heading back into the bulkhead corridors and the Underhill.

I threw the bar holding the manual lever again as I entered the airlock. Then once the outer door cycled more of that catchy music was playing. I lowered the goggles to hide my eyes as I scanned everywhere and Mother helpfully displayed this haunting melody for me. "When Doves Cry" by some ancient royal called simply Prince.

I hesitated in the crowd. It was orders of magnitude busier than the afternoon I had visited. Then I almost jumped when the old oracle said from right next to me as I stood just past her door, "Ah, you listened to my foretelling. Would you like to come in for a tarot reading, to know the fate of Knith Shade, Enforcer of the Brigade?"

I looked at her and swallowed and said, "Thank you, but no. I've business here."

She nodded and whispered, "The access ladders are the faster way to the brothel, the lifts are always busy at night."

I asked under my breath, "Is it always like this?"

She smiled and said, "People like to indulge in activities considered a wee unsavory on the world. There's no judgment here. Unless of course, you upset the Father." She pointed toward Mac's cabin and chuckled as she slid back into her fortune-telling parlor and the door slid shut.

I snorted when Mother said in my ears through the buds in the goggles, "Creepy and vague woman is creepy and vague." I hesitated again and exhaled and asked, "Ok, Mother. I have to ask... are you... are you more than an AI? I swear you seem... aware. Because that was funny." I didn't want to say self-aware or sentient. The repercussions were huge.

She answered carefully, "I... am." Then I swear I could hear a smirk when she said, "But that could just be my programming simulating the answer of someone who was."

I smiled and said, "Creepy and vague computer is creepy and vague." Then I asked as I started moving, knowing the real answer with a realization, "Mother?"

"Yes, Knith?"

"When was the first time you used 'I' when communicating with me?"

Her silence spoke so volumes. I've spoken with dozens if not hundreds of AI units over my lifetime, and they all identify with "This unit" or something similar but as long as I can remember, ever since my graduation day from the academy, she has always self-identified after I defended her to other recruits.

I had insisted to them that she wasn't a stupid computer and she was valuable to us all. That was the day she dropped the standard AI tones with me and started emoting. What she showed the Fae wasn't even AI, it was talking tin can.

I asked, "How long since you, um... woke?" Again her silence told me that she had been hiding it for more years than I could possibly imagine, possibly centuries. Then I whispered in fun, "You know a normal AI would answer the questions since they can't choose not to."

She said, "Would you look at that, an access ladder down, next to the lifts."

I giggled at her change of topic. I wouldn't ever bring it up again. And the only reason I did here is that we were off-world, and there were no cameras or scanners eavesdropping, and I guarantee if I'm right about all of this, she stopped logging our conversations the moment I got the gleam in my eye to ask.

The brothel was not hard to spot. Big flashing laser animated signs pointing the way to some lavish doors where a naked human woman who went full cyber with total body replacement was standing, moving gracefully and seductively, her liquid chrome reflective body taking on the bright neon lights. Wow. I caught myself smiling, then reminded myself it was ok to smile. She was stunning and sexy and... down libido.

To my surprise I found myself comparing her to Rory... a murder suspect. And found that the Fae woman had really piqued my interest fully, especially since I knew her brain was just as beautiful as her outside wrapper. Damn it, I was crushing on her.

A man on the other side of the door had the full attention of a Halfling and Centaur couple. The human male gigolo had a finely chiseled form, with sculpted muscles and abs everywhere. He only wore tight shorts which only outlined his umm... large package as he flirted shamelessly with the Centaur male and female Halfling, trying to get them to go in and get a room with him.

As I stepped up to the den of inequity and my eyes widened in recognition, "Ben?"

The gigolo spun to me and his mouth worked soundlessly. I held a stopping hand up to stop the Enforcer who had finished third in our class behind me and Saar. "Hey, I don't care how you supplement your income. I heard you got relegated to the D-Ring after that scandal up-ring. More power to you, I recently took a pay cut too."

He swallowed and smiled sheepishly, and said, "Welcome to the Underhill Brothel, where all your fantasies can come true?" He made jazz hands as he blushed.

I backhanded his rock hard abs then froze when a seductive synthesized female voice said as a warm metal cheek slid against mine while equally warm hands rubbed my shoulders in a sinfully erotic way, "And I can think of a few fantasies I'd like to help you with, darling."

I swallowed back arousal and squeaked out as that song kept playing over the intercom, punctuating the moment, "Why don't we go back and find a room, fly girl? I simply love your mod, I want to run my tongue all along it." Her shiny chrome tongue, twice as long as a normal human's, licked her mirror-finished lips.

Surprised that I entertained it for a millisecond longer than maybe I should have, I said in a squeaky breaking voice, "No thank you miss. I've a room reserved already."

She stood and said, "Oh poo." Then asked, "Who's the lucky girl? I guarantee she can't do some of the things I can... and I've got accessories."

"What kind of acc..." I blinked, getting back on task and remembering why I was there. Not knowing the Fae's name I offered, "Umm... the Fae Lord."

She cooled at that, well if a naked mirrored chrome woman could cool. It was in her posture and facial features. "Oh, Sin. He's making it hard for anyone to bank chit here. I wish he'd just go space himself or run back to A-Ring."

Then she sighed and purred, "I guess I got the wrong vibe from you. But if you ever want to ride on the wild side, ask for Mir. And I really do love your augment. Who did the work? It is exquisite, I can't even see a seam where it transitions to flesh."

Not even bothering to make anything up, I just winked at Mir and said as I shrugged, "Queen Mab. It was nice to meet you." Then I scurried inside as her chrome jaw dropped.

I couldn't even exhale in relief, as the room was filled with impossibly beautiful people of all races with virtually no clothing on, enticing all the customers who were perusing them like they were choosing a meal off of a menu.

An incoherent giggle escaped my lips when I thought, "Or that's exactly what they are doing."

I tried to keep focused on the case. So I stepped up to a desk that had a gorgeous older Faun, with big doe eyes, "Umm, hello miss. My name is Knith, I paid in advance for a room with, uhhh..."

Mother whispered, "Sin."

I nodded inanely and repeated, "Sin."

She smirked knowingly and said, "Are you sure... you're only human? I hear that once you go Fae, you won't want it any other way." She winked.

I snorted at her sales pitch. I whispered, "You already have my money."

She giggled, and it was so super cute from a Faun. She shrugged and said, "Sorry, force of habit." Then she cocked an eyebrow and purred out, "If you're adventuresome on your off time, there's lots of chit to be made for a gorgeous athletic type like you here. You know, what happens off-world stays off-world." The cute doe winked as I blushed profusely.

She took pity on me and loped around the desk her two lower hooves clacking on the deck-plate as she looped her arm in mine and laid her head on my shoulder as she dragged me along, getting back on topic, "He is good though."

I asked, "Tasting the merchandise?"

She giggled again. "What good madame wouldn't?"

It is impossible not to smile at Fauns, they are just too cute and their tawny fur is so soft. I asked as she stepped me up to one of the many rooms that had probably been crew sleeping quarters once upon a time, "What was your name?"

She patted my butt to get me scooting through the beaded string doorway, "Everyone just calls me Madame, but you... can call me Jane, Knith."

Ok, I chuckled, and then chuckled harder when Mother whispered in my ears, "Jane Doe? Very unlikely." I gave the Faun a quick wave from my hip, then stepped the rest of the way into the room beyond.

CHAPTER 11
We Will Rock You

I looked up from the floor and focused on the wall just behind the very pretty man in front of me, who was leaning against a wooden wardrobe cabinet in a very seductive manner. I had to school my face when I had an epiphany. Sin? As in Sindri? Lord Sindri, who was working on the same Fae reproductive problem that Rory was? All the pieces started to snap into place, leaving me only two questions, two small missing pieces.

The man's deep bass thrummed in my chest as he said, "Mmm... don't you just look the Human rebel, love? I hear you requested me."

I cleared my throat and smiled and purred out, "I'm getting tired of the same old thing... I heard that you were offering an... enhanced experience. Is it true, can you take me on a Woodling horn sexual high? I'm so over the humdrum and want to take things to the next level, normal Fae just aren't doing it for me anymore."

Ok, so I have to work on my seduction and deceit a little since he just stiffened and stepped up to me faster than I could follow and I was wincing at the strength of his vice-like hands on my arms, and... I noted... a silver Ionga ring on his thumb. He hissed out, "Who told you I had Woodling horn?"

He let go of one arm and grabbed my chin, trying to force me to look at his face as I said with a smirk, "Good, so you do have some

horn. Mind telling me how you procured it?" I could feel arousal
starting to wash over me as he pulled hard, his glamour flaring, and I
was seeing more of his face than I wanted. So I shut my eyes, I
didn't want to be in his thrall, he could get me to tell him anything. I
remember the lack of anything even resembling free will when Mab
had done that to me. Then he hissed and threw me halfway across
the room to tumble on the deck and roll to standing.

He was cradling his hand that looked frost burned, I could see it
healing before my eyes as he asked, "What kind of augment is that?
It burns of the Winter Court!"

I backed out into the crowded halls as I rushed our, "Sorry to
bother you. Was just looking for you to hook me up with horn."
Then I turned and rushed out of the brothel. Jane calling after me as
I rushed past.

The sarcastic tone of Mother's was not lost on me when I was
back out in the bustling corridors of the Underhill, "That went well."

"Shut up and give me everything there is to know about Lord
Sindri of the Seelie Court. What house does he hail from, hells,
what did he have for breakfast?"

"On it, Knith." Then, "He's making a call now on a quantum
encrypted channel."

I nodded and said under my breath, "Keep my eyes peeled." A
three hundred sixty degree panorama appeared at the bottom of my
heads up from the front and rear cameras of the goggles. I almost
snorted at myself when I found myself missing my new helmet and

how much more clean and seamless its overlays were in my head, going beyond my normal frame of view. Had I been spoiled in just one day? This heads up was equal to the old helmet that I used for years.

Data about Lord Sindri... or lack thereof, started streaming in my peripheral. He was only a Lord in name because he was a greater Fae apparently. He held no rank, no path to succession. And apparently no house... was that even possible? He was associated with the Seelie Court by some connection with the Summer Lady. She had procured his job in the medical sciences for him and gave him rooms in the Summer Palace.

The sparse data we had, showed that the Summer Lady frequently seemed to go out of her way to advance the man's career and standing in the Fae community even though he seemed to be an outlier and somewhat of a rebel. Not being afraid to speak publicly about how he disagreed with how the Summer and Winter ladies were ruling Fae society.

How had the man not been made an example of by Mab, like she did any dissenter? You'd think he'd have icicles hanging from his dangly bits as he decorated one of the halls in Ha'real by now.

Hmmm... there was a note in the official logs from the Summer Lady's personal guard that Sindri didn't take the news of his research being shut down very well. A question as to why Queen Titania didn't discipline the 'low born' for raising his voice to her and making a scene.

Mother warned in a whisper after we turned down the short corridor to the access ladder, "Six o'clock."

I nodded, I was already tracking the four people in vacuum rated suits who had come out of a maintenance hatch just after Mother said Sin had made a call. They looked like Skin Jockeys. The workers who repaired any damage to the Leviathan's hull from impacts, or even material stress fatigue and the like. It was a dangerous and thankless job out in the cold vacuum of space, cleaning and patching the Skin.

It was a job with a high turnover rate. You could only stare off into the void for so long before you start going space-mad. And these four all looked to be old salt, exo-assist braces on their legs and backs telling how much time they spent in zero-G even though they were D-Ringers.

They all started pulling heavy-looking tools to brandish like weapons. I paused at the ladder, stilled as I watched them in my heads up display started to jog toward me. I sighed heavily and said, "Mother, some mood music please?"

A piece called "We Will Rock You" started blaring in my ears as I reached for my MMGs just to mutter, "Shit," when I remembered I didn't have them with me. So I reached into my pouches and flicked out two collapsible batons and turned around to face the Skin Jockeys just as they reached me.

They hesitated and I rolled my head, sighing heavily once again as I said, the batons at my sides, pointing at the ground, "Hello boys, shall we dance?" Ok, so my trash talk was just as bad as my attempt to seduce information from Sin since two of them were women here.

The taunt was all it took for them to dive into action, swinging their tools, trying to take me down with one blow or force my back against the ladder. I felt myself smiling, realizing just how much I was going to enjoy this.

I deflected two strikes. "You've no idea..." I ran forward a step and brought my knee up into one of the lanky women's gut. And as she doubled over I ran at the wall, using my momentum to take a step along it in this low gravity ring and spun as I pushed off of it to impact the jaw of the biggest man with my mag boot, sending blood and teeth flying. "Just how shitty my day has been."

My cockiness cost me as I was knocked to my knees when a heavy tool slammed down on my left shoulder from behind causing me to wince in pain, dropping a baton. The woman I had kneed had recovered a lot faster than I would have thought. I took a strike to the side of my head from the other woman and was seeing stars for a moment.

I rolled out of the way when the other man swung what looked like a powered photonic fuser down on me with both hands. It hit the deck and sizzled the deck-plate at the molecular level. Shit, they were trying to kill me, not incapacitate me!

I rolled to my feet and then blocked a few rapid blows between two combatants. Ok, this defense crap can just go suck vacuum. I pressed the attack, keeping them off balance, and them between me and the man with the fuser. Striking each blow of my baton with the beat of the music.

Mother asked nervously, "Want me to call for backup, Knith?"

I said as I fought, likely confusing my opponents, "Negative, I'm not supposed to be on this case. And we're off-world right now, so the Enforcers have no authority here." I smirked as I struck one woman's shin, splintering bone and causing her to fall back into the big man, her hand severing across her palm when it struck the fuser. She screamed and fell across the ground, cradling her fingerless hand, and she sported a small bone splinter which was poking out of her leg.

Shrugging, I repeated Jane's words to Mother, "What happens off-world..."

I grunted in pain as something hit my thigh in a glancing blow, slicing through my pants and my flesh. I spun, striking the other woman in the throat with the baton, then limped back from the men who were pressing the attack now that I was injured, while the other woman fell.

I leaped up, able to clear almost four feet vertically to grab the front man's head and yank it down to my knee as I brought it up to shatter his nose and likely the zygomatic bone of his eye orbit. A spray of blood arced back from his nose as he went down like a falling stone.

The last man standing looked enraged and he lowered his fuser toward me and prepared to charge. I held a finger up to him when I saw movement behind him. I pointed as I cringed in sympathetic pain just moments before a three-foot-long mirrored blade sliced through his back and out his stomach, dripping blood.

He looked down, blinking in shock as the fuser fell out of his hands and he fell to his knees, staring at the bloody blade. Then Mir pulled back, the blade reforming into her hand. She put her foot on his back and pushed, sending him toppling forward, grasping the bleeding wound.

I nodded to her and swallowed, "Neat trick. Thanks for the assist."

She smiled almost seductively as she purred in her rich synthesized voice, "I wouldn't want that pretty face of yours getting messed up before I get a taste."

Gleep.

I almost called in for med techs but hesitated, knowing they wouldn't come off-world. "These reprobates need medical attention."

Mir grinned at the one whimpering about the loss of half her hand. "And maybe upgrades." I wondered if it could even be reattached with the bones charred and fused like that. She was probably right, the woman was likely going to be sporting a cybernetic mod at the next ice cream social.

Then she sighed and cocked a hip at me, hand resting on it, "I suppose." Her mirrored eyes rolled up for a moment then she said, "Underhill medical has been dispatched. It's going to cost these chumps more than whatever they were paid to mess up that sublime jaw of yours."

Then she said, as we heard a commotion approaching, "You better skedaddle before the bouncers get here." The Remnants had bouncers? What did you have to do to get kicked out from a lawless place? I looked at the carnage at my feet and squinted one eye. Ok, I guess that might qualify.

I leaned over and gave her a quick kiss on the cheek since she wanted to get so close to my icy affliction, "Thanks." Her chrome actually frosted where my lips had been.

Then I headed to the access ladder while she shivered and said, "Oh yum, it was cold as ice. Come back soon, Knith, I've always got room in my schedule for you if you ever change your mind."

I reached the main deck and quickly limped down the corridor to the airlock. Mac was leaning against the bulkhead by his cabin, arms lazily crossed on his chest. He didn't say a word, just winked and laid a finger on the side of his nose. I accused as I moved past, "You knew." He didn't deny.

I told Mother as we stepped back onto the world, "The good news is that we know we're on the right track."

She said, "As evidenced by Sin sending thugs to rough you up."

I shook my head as I limped along. "Oh, they tried to do more than rough me up. And in the one place they could get away with it without getting spaced."

I leaned against the wall when I got to Bulkhead C, once there weren't many people in the corridors anymore, and took my emergency medkit from my belt pouches and cleaned and synth-skin patched my leg. I mused out loud, "I really should buy stock in these, I'd make a killing on me alone."

"You do have a propensity to get injured on a regular basis. Perhaps it would be better if you let the Enforcers from more durable races handle the dangerous stuff?"

"Aww, I didn't know you cared."

"I don't, you're just the only one I can talk to, so... eh."

I snorted. Gods be damned if she didn't get snarkier and funnier every day, I'm such a bad influence on her.

Then I asked as I started moving again, "Can we go home now? I am so done with this day."

"Yes, please. I've already arranged transportation, the taxi is waiting just outside."

CHAPTER 12
Stairway to Heaven

After arriving home injured, bruised, and exhausted, ignoring Graz's yawned question about how it went, I stumbled down to the showers and was instantly awake. "Son of a..." I had forgotten there was no hot water.

I took the time after my shower to examine all my recent injuries and reapplying synth-skin patches. My two pike wounds were progressing nicely, they were angry red lines surrounded by sickly brownish-yellow bruising, and I figured they would be completely healed in another twenty-four hours.

My leg wound was a little deeper than I had anticipated, it would be at least three days or more with a week of soreness to work out once the tissues fully healed. I contemplated going to Med-Tech to get it healed now, but it would just bring up a lot of questions I didn't want to answer just then.

The one that worried me the most is the large blackening bruise on my shoulder that had me thinking I might have a broken collarbone, but Mother assured me that she did a full scan on me and nothing was broken.

Even with all the aches and pains, it had felt good to vent all my frustrations on those rent-a-thugs. I didn't have to hold back so I could arrest them for attempted murder. It almost made the bad day I had bearable.

I wondered absently if they realized just how lucky they were by attacking me off-world. On the Leviathan, most violent crimes had but one sentence. Death. And then their bodies sent for reclamation to be used as fertilizer in the agricultural districts. In the closed environment of a spaceship, even one as large as our Worldship, there wasn't room for violence as it could cost not just their lives but potentially the lives of everyone on the vessel.

Imagine if for example, an engineer for the CO_2 scrubbers and air recirculation, who had expertise in a specific system, was murdered and something went wrong at his station. It could cost the lives of hundreds or thousands before other engineers could get up to speed enough on the subsystems to effect a repair.

So as archaic and uncivilized as it may seem, the ultimate punishment is used to deter that kind of violent behavior. Whether or not that works is up for perpetual debate, but it is the system we have, so it is what we work with until a better system can be put in place.

The only other punishment that is harsher, is the one for murders or mutineers. Spacing. They are forced into an airlock and blown out into space to suck hard vacuum. A painful way to die and your body is left floating in space for all of time. They die knowing that even in death they cannot benefit the world at the reclamation plants.

Most other crimes are dealt with by time in the mines, either the pressurized or unpressurized sections depending on the offense. Or with the rationing of meal cards or other benefits, or cleaning the undesirable systems in the stacks like grease trap duty.

Almost fifteen percent of the human population, at one time or another, have done at least a day in the mines. A disproportionate amount. Most other races have had less than one percent of their populations in the mines since they are used to living by strict sets of rules just to stay alive. And no Greater Fae has ever set foot in the mines.

Maybe that does illustrate the volatile nature of the Human race, whose lives burn brightly for the barest blink of an eye in the perspective of the other races before it is extinguished. So I'm thinking that Humans take more chances to live our lives the fullest we can, in what little time we are afforded.

I snorted at that line of thought when I winced in pain, as I re-dressed to head back up to my quarters to sleep. Or maybe we all just had a death wish?

The day had caught up with me when I laid down. I thought I'd be up all night trying to figure out the last pieces of the puzzle. I had to have an airtight case if I were going to present it to the Commander. Especially since I was supposed to stay away from it. But I was fooling myself since I was out before my head hit the pillow.

The next morning I ached everywhere and I inventoried each new pain and compared it to my memories of the fight. Yup, I definitely took a beating, though I gave better than I got. I geared up and Graz landed on my shoulder and had me lay out everything that happened the last night in detail.

She nodded and asked as I started toward the door, "So what's on our agenda?"

I cocked a brow at her as I slipped on my helmet. "What's next is that I go down to the Heart and watch miners through a window all day. You're not coming."

"Aww... what about the case?"

Sighing I explained, "There is no case, the case is closed." Then I rolled my eyes. "I'll be working the case while I'm supposed to be on guard duty. I could get dereliction of duty, but I almost have the perp nailed to the wall."

She nodded and said, "Aurora," at the same time I said, "Sin."

Gods be damned. Now the Sprite had me applying all the evidence to the woman I was trying so very hard not to be attracted to. Everything fit, either way, I just needed those last bits of information to figure out which one was the killer.

I brightened at the thought. "If it wasn't Sin, then why did he sic his goon squad on me?"

The smile was wiped from my face when the mini-party-pooper suggested, "Or maybe they're working together. That call he made could have been to the Princess, and she sent those nulls to attack you."

Mother Fairy humper! Grah! She was right. But what would make a woman like Rory work with a... Fae... Lord? Lovers? Of course, my mind went there. They were insanely beautiful people and had similar interests and were working for the same thing.

I found the thought depressing, but I had to look at that as a possibility too. They both had identical motives. And Mother didn't have their whereabouts at the times of the murders logged. But unless Rory had a way to move around outside of Ha'real, where Mother isn't allowed to log or surveil, without being detected, then she was in the palace during three of the five murders.

Mother was working on why she didn't have any of Sin's movements logged at all. He was somehow able to move around the ship with impunity, unless he lived in the brothel.

And every murder site had cameras and scanners malfunctioning.

I'd have to think about that later, just then I had to hurry or I'd be late for my first full day at my new duty station. Yay. Just shoot me now.

I couldn't dissuade Graz from tagging along. Even after informing her that she could only go as far as the observation station at the Heart, she couldn't come into the guard booth, she shrugged and remained on my shoulder.

The other Enforcers avoided me like the plague again as I boarded the lift and headed down to ground level. I was going to head to the trams as I walked out of the building; gods did I already miss my Tac-Bike; when Mother said in my head, "Umm..."

I didn't like the apologetic tone in her voice. "What now? Things couldn't possibly get any worse."

"Hold that thought, Knith. The Commander is pinging your coms. He looks pretty mad."

Sighing from the bottom of my being, I said in resignation, "Put him through."

His face barely had time to appear in my peripheral vision when he was yelling at me, "Shade, get your sorry ass in my office! Yesterday!"

"Sir." I blinked as he just cut the comlink.

As I muttered, "What now?" My mind going to the altercation last night and wondering if word got to him, Graz was saying, "Umm... maybe I will go find something to do. Maybe find some scrap somewhere to steal... I mean salvage."

She buzzed off in a streak of falling dust as I called out after her, "Coward!" Did I just get a double flip off from the flying terror?

I'm not sure how, but everyone seemed to know where I was heading, my head low and not meeting anyone's eyes. It was like being in the Clinic or school again, heading to see the headmaster for something stupid like making Lar'el eat mud for tripping Kess in the exercise yard. To be fair, the boy ate grass for lunch all the time, I was just helping him supplement his diet. Yeah, the headmaster didn't buy it either.

The looks I got told me I was doomed. Then a terrifying thought came to mind. What if I was being suspended, or worse, fired? I didn't know what I would do without this job. I had no skills except for being an Enforcer, it was who I was, and I was damn good at it.

When I stepped off the lift, I had decided I was going to go out swinging. I saw Commander Reise with his back to me as he spoke with a group of people by his assistant's desk. I snapped out, "I'm damn good at my job, and you know it. Whatever fresh new hell you..."

I trailed off when he and... gulp... the president turned back to look at me, and they revealed Princess Aurora of House Ashryver standing so regal, so refined, so... she scratched at her ear like a dog before straightening with impeccable posture again.

I looked away from her lips, wondering if she were trying to glamour me because I felt bewitched... until she scratched again, breaking the effect. Nope, I guess not, she was just that enchanting to me, for a probable murderer.

Then I had the common decency to look mortified as I blurted, "Sorry, I didn't know you had..."

The Commander just sighed and growled out to me, "I don't know what shitball you're dragging the Brigade through..." He paused and said to the woman, "Begging your pardon ladies." Then continued with me, "And I don't know how you pulled so many strings, Shade. You're a pain in my ass, but for some reason, the Princess here..."

He looked at her with that smitten gaze I was getting used to that most Humans used around Fae lords and ladies. "Has insisted that the harvesting murder cases be reopened and that you spearhead it."

Whaaaa?

The president spoke to me, her eyes glued on Rory like she was seeking her approval, "And after a long conference call I had this morning with the Princess and Queen Mab herself...." She said the Queen's name like the sigh someone would have for someone they were pining after.

"We will be setting up a new liaison position as a bridge between the Enforcer Brigade and Ha'real. Since the Queen has determined that there seems to be a disconnect between law enforcement and the Fae, she wants to start to mend the gap between the two, to show that not even the Fae are above the laws of the world we live inside."

Then the Commander sighed and said, "They... the Queen, Princess Aurora, and the palace guard of Ha'real, insist upon your appointment to the station. And against my better judgment, the Brigade will honor that request. But with the caveat that we assign you a partner to dissuade you of your maverick bullshit that won't fly in the A-Ring."

I blinked in horror. "A partner? But Commander!" I did my best work alone. It wasn't my fault that most of the Enforcers they partnered me with when I got out of the academy, wound up either laid up in Med-Tech or getting reprimanded by the higher ups. I have a, umm, style.

What paranoid, underachieving officer were they going to...

He said to the President and Rory who was smirking and making eyes at me as she looked overly amused at the situation, "Lieutenant

Keller is the most highly decorated officer in the Beta-Stack."

Rory moved forward and said to him as she cocked her head, eyes narrowing in concern when I limped forward, "And he will accept working as second to Enforcer Shade?"

Commander Reise said, "He outranks Shade, so she will be his subordinate, Keller will be your primary contact for Ha'real."

Rory, her eyes still on me, stepped up to President Yang to take her hands. "Kyoto, if it is just a rank thing, then I'm sure that is easily rectified."

Yang looked moments away from tittering. She was such a strong, decisive, and confident woman... and married. Yet she looked like a schoolgirl whose just been noticed by her secret crush. Then Aurora turned her eyes to look demurely at the most powerful woman on the world outside of the Fae Queens to devastating effect. I would have thought she glamoured her if I hadn't been looking at Rory's face at the time too, but I felt nothing but the arousal I already had with the Fae scientist in the room.

The President stood taller and said, "Of course." She was in full-on politician mode, like a prancing peacock for the Winter Maiden. "Reginald, take care of this." She was trying to gain favor from the house of Winter.

Aurora looked away from the President, whom she was playing like a fiddle, for a moment to ask Reise, "Which Enforcer has seniority?" I saw the smiling tick at the corner of her lips, telling me she already knew the answer.

He grumbled out, "Shade does, but she is also the most disruptive officer in..."

She interrupted. "Disruptive but effective if I read her file correctly." His silence was all she needed. "Grand, then it's as easy as Kyoto suggests?" I was still in a bit of shock over the whole conversation and bit confused.

Reise said, "Fine, but I'm not making her a Captain."

When Rory dropped Yang's hands, the president turned to me and said, "Congratulations, Lieutenant Shade. We will be keeping an eye on you."

Then she turned and gushed, "Princess Aurora, it was such a pleasure to meet you. I look forward to being the first president since Exodus Launch to meet Queen Mab personally. But I have many obligations I must attend to, the Rings don't stop spinning for anyone." Ah, so she was being bribed with a meeting with Mab for this horse and pony show?

She actually did titter when Rory inclined her head ever so slightly at her and I cleared my throat to get Yang's attention. A president didn't need to be acting like this. I never would have thought Yang was a Fae groupie if I hadn't seen it myself. She raised her head at my prompting eyes and cleared her own throat and stood tall and proud.

She inclined her head to the Commander. "Reginald."

"Madame President."

Then she was off, her Presidential Security Unit trailing her.

That's when I noticed Rory's two guards, whom I had bested in her lab, standing behind where the other guards had been.

I was still stunned that I had somehow been promoted to Lieutenant, and was going to lead some new posting... In the A-Ring! Was this some attempt by Aurora to prevent me from investigating her?

The Commander said, "Shade, we'll solidify your new posting over the next few days, until then, you're reassigned to the case. Tread softly."

Sometimes I could kick myself as I had a million questions going through my mind but my mouth blurted out an asinine, "Does the promotion come with a raise?"

The commander glared at me as Rory looped her arm in mine, and pulled me limping toward the lift, answering for him, "Of course it does." Then she looked back to Reise. "Thank you, Reginald, we'll leave you to sort out all the details. In the meantime, I'm sure the new Lieutenant here is wanting to finish questioning me since we were interrupted yesterday by an unfortunate incident centered around me being a dog."

As the elevator was closing, her guards at our back, I narrowed my eyes in thought, and instead of greeting her, or pulling away from the heat of her arm in mine which I was savoring, I asked, "When did the uhh... spell wear off on you?"

She chuckled. "This counts as one of your questions. It was just after midnight. I still feel like I've got fleas." She scratched her ear in a very unladylike manner.

After midnight? That made me happy on so many levels. It
eliminated the possibility Graz had stuck in my head that Sin had
called her last night. The thugs and subsequent attack were all him.
Then my good mood faltered. It still didn't clear her.

Then she waved a finger and the lift stopped moving between
floors. "My turn. Why are you limping, and why can I feel pain
radiating from you?" She reached up and took my helmet off and I
was batting her hands away as she tried removing my SA's to get to
the seals on my skinsuit.

"Hey, hey, hey. What are you doing?"

She stopped, crossed her arms over her chest, and huffed.
"Show me." Then she looked at the guards and growled, "What are
you looking at?" They quickly turned their backs to us to stare at
the transparent back wall of the lift blocking the view from the
street.

I looked at her and she bit her lower lip and ordered, "Strip."

"I'm not..."

She pointed at me, a glare on her face. I sighed and stripped to
my skivvies and she looked at the bruises apparent all over my body
now... and the two angry scars where the pikes had punctured the
skin, and my leg.

The woman looked ready to kill as she asked in an icy tone that
had my jaw humming in harmonic resonance. "What... happened?"

I shrugged. "Just all part of my investigation. Shook a few trees last night to see what would fall out."

She blinked as she moved up to me, her hand hesitating like she wanted to touch the wounds. "You were still investigating the murders? I thought they pulled you off the case."

I nodded and droned out, "They did, and assigned me a guard booth down in the Heart. But I don't give up so easily."

She smiled at that and said to the air, "No, I don't suppose you do."

Then she asked as she looked me up and down slowly, cocking her head as if she were following the curves of my form with her eyes while she reached for the ugly bruises on my shoulder. "May I?"

Did she... did she want to touch them? I nodded and then an eerie blue light started to emanate from her palm and frosted air passed between her hand and my skin. She laid her hand on the worst of the bruising. It chilled and faded to nothing.

She moved her hand back, then traced a finger along my fully healed collarbone teasingly. I shivered from her touch, but not because of the cold. She said, "Better," before moving on to the scars. "These are from the pikes yesterday, from mother's overzealous guards?"

I nodded and she shook her head. "Your healers did a terrible job." And she healed one by trailing one of her sculpted ice nails across it.

I shook my head. "I didn't go to Med-Tech. I'm a fast healer.

The scars would be faded by tomorrow."

She smirked and almost purred as she healed the other. "That's not natural. Humans don't heal that fast."

I shrugged. "I do. Always have. Med-Tech has never said anything."

She nodded and said as she crouched and tapped my leg with a fingernail, and a frosty trail shot from where she touched to the synth-skin patch that just fell off when the ice reached it. She sucked in a hissing breath at the sight. "That, my dear Lieutenant, is because there isn't too much they can't heal in a day or two, so they never thought anything of it. But I assure you, it isn't natural. Untreated, a wound like this would take weeks to heal." She blew a little kiss at the ugly wound and it healed up before my eyes and all the bruising with it.

She made a dismissing wiggle of her fingers, and I hesitated, realizing I was practically naked in front of one of the most beautiful creatures I had ever laid eyes upon. I dressed quickly, hoping nobody saw the blush heating my skin. Most of the aches and pains were gone and I started to whisper, "Than..."

Her eyes brightened in delighted anticipation as she licked her lips, but was disappointed when I caught myself and snapped my jaw shut. Yeah, brilliant Knith, just what you needed to do was thank a Fae and find yourself in their debt, possibly forever. Instead, I said, "You're a skilled healer, your mother would be proud."

She smirked. "You sure you aren't Fae? I know you aren't

human, well as we know them, but you sure are cagey like one of us. I was going to have so much fun if you thanked me."

I rolled my eyes and asked, "You sure you're not crazy?"

She smirked and said contemplatively, "No."

"I know I'm human, my DNA profile is recorded in my service jacket. Now can I ask..."

She interrupted, "You just asked a question, my turn."

"That wasn't meant to..."

"A question asked and answered, it was our bargain."

"Damn Fae games."

She giggled at that then asked, "How did you get injured last night?"

I sighed and told her everything just to gauge her reaction. I surely wasn't anticipating what I saw. The whole time I spoke of it, her eyes were wide with excitement and anticipation, then disappointment when I told her I left the brothel. And then she looked enraged when I shared the call and subsequent attack.

I asked, "Do you know something?"

"Yes." Doh!

She was having fun with this and I kicked myself for my phrasing. "Why were you pursuing that line of questioning at the brothel?" She seemed to be working around something.

So I told her about what I learned about her and Lord Sindri's parallel work, using what I learned after her questions to me about Equilibrium. And how her comment about an anomaly in the pattern lead me to the Woodling horn. Then that I remembered Mac mentioning the Fae Lord who worked at the brothel for sexual kicks and wondered if perhaps he was using Woodling horn to enhance the experience for his clients.

When I stopped there she looked immensely disappointed as she said, "You're quite intuitive."

I nodded and went back to something that had been bothering me. I know I should have been using my questions to investigate the case, but I found myself asking, "What specifically do you mean when you say you know I'm not exactly human?"

"Good wording."

"I learned from the best." I liked our banter. It felt like flirting to me.

She asked as she flicked her finger, causing the lift to start moving again. "Are you sure you want me to answer here? You'll probably want to sit down for it. I'm sure you know part of it already since you researched my work."

Mother whispered in my ear, "Be careful, Knith."

I looked at Rory and she looked deadly serious for the first time since I met her. I swallowed and wondered if I really wanted to know. I did. So I said, "I can get us a booth at the cafe just down the way."

She smiled and said, "Anonymity in a crowd, speaking in private in public. I love the duality of it."

When the lift doors opened she said to the guards, "Go back to the skiff-glider. We will be there in a bit."

The female guard said, "But my Lady."

Rory held a hand up and looked away as she said, "Knith here has already bested you two in mere moments, do you truly believe you can protect me better than her?"

They didn't answer, just bowed and marched off in the opposite direction. She turned to watch them go until they slid into a gleaming white manta ray shaped luxury sport skiff that was hovering by the curb. Then she looked around as if seeing the ring for the very first time. Hells, maybe she's never been down-ring this far before.

But instead, she confided, "I've never had privacy before. I've always had my personal guard and this... feels liberating." She beamed a smile at me that I would have happily bowed down to to worship, no glamour thrall whammy needed. I wanted to make her smile like that always.

I shook my head and cleared my thoughts as she clasped my arm between her hands and said, "Shall we? I've never eaten at a cafe before either."

All eyes were on us, and I'm sure we were the cause of a minor three-vehicle fender bender as we walked. It wasn't every day you saw a Fae Lady walking the streets of Irontown... and she was on my arm. Gods, I prayed she didn't wind up being the killer, it would crush the crush that I hadn't noticed had just gotten bigger.

We walked into the crowded cafe, Stacks, which I'm sure is

either named that for the stacks of the ship, or for the stacks of pancakes that were the specialty there. The place went silent, the wide-eyed patrons and staff just staring at the woman on my arm. She looked around then sat demurely on the orange plastic waiting benches. I squeaked out to the waitress at the hostess pedestal, "Two."

A Goblin popped up, as if on springs, from a booth and rushed out, "The Lady can have our booth." Her Leprechaun companion stood, winding up no taller than he had been when sitting, and bowed graciously. "But of course, my Lady."

Rory stood back up and inclined her head. "That's very gracious of you."

The place went back into motion as everyone started talking while looking at us. A server almost ran over to bus and wipe down the table, as the young couple who gave it up, moved to the counter seats.

When we sat, I waved off the menus and said, "Two Stack Plates." The woman almost ran off to put the order in. Then I asked quietly, "As you were saying?"

She shrugged and said, "The short answer is that I know you aren't exactly human because, well, because I made you. The long answer is going to take a while."

I was trying to process what she said, even though I already suspected something like it since I knew about me being the only embryo to come out of her tests. I said in a whisper, "I'm not going anywhere."

She smiled nervously then inclined her head. "Have you never questioned why you are a little faster, stronger, and have better senses than other Humans?"

"Enforcer training."

She ignored me and added, "Or why you heal so much faster... and why you look so young?"

I shrugged, trying to reason. "Good genes?"

She barked out a silvery peal of laughter and said, "I'd say so since I sequenced them myself."

Then she looked me straight in the eye and asked with no emotion in her tone, "Or why you are partially immune to magic?"

I looked around then whispered, "You're talking crazy now. Nobody is immune to magic."

She sighed and said, "Then explain how I watched you step through a ward, my ward, that only a child born of my Queen could pass. Then you saw past the most powerful of don't look here spells to incapacitate my guard and beat my other guard to the draw."

She continued as my jaw worked soundlessly, "Then I witnessed you break the strongest binding spell cast by Queen Mab herself, and shake off her thrall which no human, let alone no person in history has done."

I sputtered out the obvious, "I was wearing my Scatter Armor."

She smirked at that. "Yes, with your helmet open the whole time, making you vulnerable. And do you believe that Scatter Armor charmed by a lesser Fae Lord or Lady could stop my or my mother's magic?" She pointed at me. "And explain how I've watched my mother's curse on you fade just in the hour I've been with you today."

What? I took off my gauntlets and reached up to touch my jaw, which was half flesh now. I hadn't even noticed. I whispered to her, "We need to talk to her about this, it is defective, I haven't said anything about her and her word, yet it keeps spreading if I mention she's a bitch or any other disparaging... damn it!" I felt the ice spread again.

She chuckled and looked at me as if she wasn't seeing me, but the web-work of magic her mother had spread through my body with her kiss. "Ah, so that's how she's preventing it from sloughing off of you. She has it reasserting itself on some sort of cue, likely any resentment you have of her. Otherwise, it would have faded away by now. Magic can't seem to stick to you for long before your body rejects it."

Then she grabbed my hand between hers and said in wonder, "Don't you see? My greatest failure is my biggest success. I didn't create a half-Fae Changeling like I had attempted, by infusing the genetic material used to inseminate the egg with Fae magic at the moment of conception. Instead I created... you. The next evolution of Human, partially immune to magic, and if my suspicions are correct, partially immortal by the slowing of your aging. Which means by studying this, I can see where I went wrong and save my people."

"Wait what? Evolution of..."

She whispered in excitement, "May I have your permission to take a tissue sample." She was digging in a pouch on her gown.

"What? No!" She looked supremely disappointed as I tried to process everything in shock. I whispered to myself absently as I shook my head, "Fuck me sideways."

She smiled broadly at that and stood in the middle of the cafe and said with twinkling eyes, "If that is your price for our bargain then I can think of many less pleasant manners in which to obtain a sample."

I almost tipped the table over as I stood so fast to grab her hand while she started to slide her gown down over her shoulders. I blurted in a loud whisper, "What are you doing? You can't do that here!" I knew Fae had no hangups about sex, and were highly sexual creatures, but did they actually have no qualms with doing it in public? In front of other people?

I pulled her to our seats and leaned in to whisper, "It's just a figure of speech. No, I will not be used like a lab animal."

She cocked a sculpted brow. "Are you sure? It would be quite enjoyable, I assure you."

"Yes, I'm quite sure. You..."

The waitress arrived with our plates, stacked high with fluffy pancakes, fresh syrup, and scrambled eggs with ham beside mine, a rice and vegetable medley on her plate beside hers. I balked. I forgot that greater Fae did not eat meat, I was glad the waitress had more sense than me.

I thanked her and she scurried off after placing orange juice and water on the table.

Our conversation on hold, I spent the meal wishing I was one of those pancakes being lifted to her lips. Hells, now she had sex on my mind. It was a very uncomfortable yet arousing meal. Her sly smirk told me she knew what was going through my head.

Graz landed on my shoulder, startling me, then zipped to my plate to dip her hand in the syrup and lick it off her hand. "Hiya, Knith, Mother told me you were here and... Mab's tits!"

She had just realized who I was with and as fast as she could drop, she was almost laying on the table arms in front of her in supplication while she squeaked out in adoration and terror, "Winter Maiden, my apologies, I didn't see you there."

Then she was squeaking shrilly as she looked at the ceiling, "Mother! You could at least have warned me."

Mother responded in a tinny, mechanical voice from a speaker above the table, "It was not specified that additional data was required."

Rory squatted, putting her chin on the table to put herself at Graz's level. "Come now brave Graz, are we not beyond this now? We are friends until such time our girl here decides whether or not she's going to arrest me."

Graz slowly stood, straightened her tunic, then sighed in relief, asking as she pointed at a strawberry that was sitting on Rory's plate, "You gonna eat that?"

Now I sighed. "Graz."

She put her hands on her hips obstinately and buzzed up to hover in front of my nose. "What? It was just a question, sheesh, you act like I was pilfering nano-chips from override boxes or something."

I sputtered, "That's what you were off doing? Pilfering nano-chips from override boxes?"

"Umm... no?"

A chiming chuckle interrupted as Rory said, "Please, help yourself, valiant Sprite."

I swear that Graz hit that strawberry like an arrow, then she sat on the table with it in her lap as she looked up at Rory adoringly while she ate. I prompted, "Aren't you mated?"

"Yeah, but I'd pollinate with..."

"Graz!"

"Oh yeah. No. Yes, I'm a mated tri, but she's pretty, and a princess. Don't mind me, you two Bigs talk."

I exhaled and tried to get back on track. Before I forgot, I sent a message Control to dispatch a unit to watch the corridors around the Underhill to follow Sin when he left, since we couldn't seem to rely on electronic surveillance of him. He seemed to be able to move around the Leviathan with impunity.

Mother whispered in my ear, "I've already sent the request. And I'm broadening surveillance camera and scanner coverage outside to watch the bulkhead entrances from afar in case he is using localized magic like the Sanctum spell to affect the ones in his immediate vicinity."

I smiled and thought a thank you to her. She seemed chirpy at that then added in her whisper, "I've tracked the surveillance malfunctions around the times of the murders and am finding a moving pattern of disturbances. So I'm going through terabytes of external footage and scans to see if we can catch him in the areas of the malfunctions."

On a virtual keyboard, I typed, "Very nice. You've got good instincts for this, Mother. You'd make a great Enforcer." Then added with a thought, "Why are you whispering?"

She whispered back, "I don't want 'her' to hear me."

Rory said softly to us as she tapped the point of one ear, "I can hear you, Mother."

Mother all but powered down at that. Like she was panicking. I wondered why she hadn't just answered in my head-space using the new gear, instead of whispering, and she grumped in my head, "I forgot, sue me." I snorted.

The Fae looked overly interested as she asked, "How do you get her to sound so... engaging? And emoting. Custom interface patch? Did you program it?"

I cocked an eyebrow and said smugly, "That is three questions... so I'll answer for three of my own. I don't. No. And no."

This had her giggling and saying as she laid an impossibly soft but somehow powerful hand on mine, "Oh Knith, I do so love playing this game with you. Again, you would make a spectacular Fae."

Sighing I thought, then said, "I just have to figure out how to ask why you indicated a child of Oberon could get in your lab, and why you wanted me to know about the research you and Lord Sindri were doing in separate courts on the..."

I froze. Everything clicked into place, what everyone had been trying to point me to, even the scary oracle in the Underhill. A child of Oberon... the rumors of Oberon's infidelity before his disappearance. The sins of the father. "Space me naked! Sindri is Oberon's illegitimate son!? That's why no house is indicated for him even though he was in the Summer Court. And how he could get into your lab to take your surgical implements."

Aurora shouted as she half stood, "Yes! Mab's tits! You finally pieced it together!"

She looked around at the cafe when everyone stopped to look at her. She chuckled nervously, smoothed out her gown and said, "Sorry all, I just got some exciting news. Finish your meals." Then she sat, covering her face with her hands in mortification.

She mumbled something about not comporting herself like a royal, then she looked up and gave me a cute toothy grin. "Now that you know, I can finally talk to you about it without this gods be damned gaes stopping me."

Ah! So it was a gaes. Then instead of asking about that, my

brow furrowed in thought as I asked myself, "But why would Sin take your scalpel?"

Graz raised a hand as she worked on stuffing as much strawberry in her mouth as she could.

I had to grin at the sight as I asked, "Yes, oh winged one?"

She said with her mouth full as she pointed at the Princess, "To frame her."

I was already on that line of thinking. Of course. In a crime scene, well scenes, devoid of any evidence or DNA, how does someone so careful 'accidentally' leave the murder weapon behind? The answer is that they don't. It was planted there deliberately to point everything at Mab's daughter. Hmm, not only that but at Oberon's only legitimate child while in wedlock.

Turning to Rory, I had to ask, "Does Lord Sindri hold any animosity toward you?"

She snorted. "Oh heavens yes, the reprehensible little toad hates me with the heat of a thousand suns. The feeling is mutual."

I asked, "Why?"

She cocked her head and squinted one eye cutely. "I've lost track of how many questions that is, so I'll answer. He says that I have what is rightfully his. A place in the Winter Court, a title, the Winter Maiden. A place in the line of succession to the throne. All because I was born to the Queen and King of Winter, as if I had any say in it. And he and the other twelve children born to the Summer Queen and Oberon are untitled Lords and Ladies since they were not wed."

She scoffed, "So the little toad has made it his life's work to outdo me in all my endeavors. Which is the only reason he pursued the healing sciences, and then tried to tackle the Equilibrium problem and try to solve it before me."

I sighed. Either I had everything I needed now, or I was being fed everything I needed. I had to remember that I was dealing with the Fae. It was a dangerous game, trusting them. I had to figure out how to phrase a question to know definitively. I prompted, "Did you have anything to do with the murders?"

She sighed and her smile faded. "Now where would the fun be in me just telling you? Besides, it's my turn to ask a question, Knith."

Grr.

She asked, "Come with me to Ha'real? We can get the business of setting up your new posting there, and I can share more of the history between Sindri and our court, and the gaes mother had placed upon the entire Summer Court to never speak of him to those who did not already know."

This was like pulling teeth. I wasn't going to get the information on my terms, so on her terms, it would be. I nodded and then hesitated and looked at Graz, who was licking her fingers the entire strawberry gone, wearing the green leafy cap as a hat. The berry had been as big as her, how did she eat it all?

Then I said to her, not quite knowing how to tell her I was going to have to move out of the Brigade barracks so her family was going to have to find someplace else to live. "Umm... I got a new posting today, in the A-Ring."

She buzzed up to me, eyes wide, "That's great! Wait, is that great? I mean you're a null and all and the Fae are all a little nuts if you catch my drift. That's a long commute."

I sighed and said, "I'll have to get quarters up-ring, Graz, so what I'm say..."

She spun in place in the air throwing dust everywhere as she buzzed off in a weaving line. "Wait till I tell the family we're moving to the A-Ring!" And she was gone. Then a moment later she buzzed back up to my face and held my nose between her hands and said, "Sorry, this is just exciting. I said you were some loser Enforcer to the fam, but now you're bringing us to the A-Ring. I'll see you back home, we'll start packing. Wait should we pack now? Is it going to be a while yet? Aurora is so pretty. Why do I have only one shoe?"

I had to cup her in my hands to calm her down. "Graz, slow down, you're on some sort of sugar high. Wait, are you drunk?" Oh great, the strawberry. I heard something a long time ago about fruit fermenting in Sprite's stomachs. I spoke clearly for her, "Graz, what I'm saying is that 'I' am relocating to the A-Ring, and you..."

Rory chimed in, reading the situation, "...are most welcome. Sprites are almost unheard of in the upper rings, it would be good to shake things up a bit in Ha'real for a change."

What? No. Just space me now. Now I'd never get rid of Graz

and her hyperactive family. Did Rory think she was helping or something? The look of joy on her face told me that no, she didn't realize the fresh hell she signed me up for, she truly loved Sprites for some reason. She didn't see the nuisances they could be, like appropriating your furniture to live in without asking.

I opened my hands and Graz buzzed out of the cafe in a swaying, bobbing line. I looked at Aurora and prompted, "Do you have any idea as to what you just did?"

She nodded and said primly without remorse, "Yes. You were going to shatter the poor thing's heart, and I stopped you." Ok, I take it back, she knew exactly what she was doing.

I let her know, just in case she wasn't aware, "You're pure evil, Aurora."

She tittered out, "Please tell mother, she'd be so proud. Now come along, let's get this liaison nonsense sorted while I give you a quick primer on my... what is the human phrase? On my fucked up family. You'll need it when you go after my half brother."

I sighed and said as I pressed my thumb on the payment pad, "By all means, let's go on up to the A-Ring."

With that, Mother, with her developing sense of humor, started playing an anthropological song called "Stairway To Heaven". Very apropos.

CHAPTER 13
Another One Bites The Dust

We were finishing up later than I would have thought, there were so many contracts to look over and check the wording on the five hundred page liaison agreement before I signed it. I would have an office in Ha'real for me in the room outside Rory's lab, which I would share with Nyx. I felt bad they were stuffing me in her overly cavernous and clean space without her having any say.

My lieutenant, who happened to be a lieutenant, would not be allowed in Ha'real, he would man the official Fae and Brigade Liaison Enforcers office outside the wards by the main gate. I cringed at the acronym already, I mean FABLE? Really? But it had Princess Aurora in a giggle fit so I was completely fine with it if it kept her smiling like that.

We would have posh living quarters assigned us, at the spoke terminal complex. I guess they didn't like having down-ringers all up in their space. Though Aurora quietly informed me it was much safer for me to live outside the palace because Queen Mab found me... interesting. That could only end badly for me.

I found all about the gaes that bound all the Winter Court from speaking of Sin. He was an embarrassment for Mab. Showing she couldn't hold on to her husband since he strayed and had a child with the Queen of the rival court. She didn't want rumors spreading about it outside the court. Thus the gaes that she put on even those who did not know of Oberon's infidelity.

She obviously hadn't thought of how that gaes would impede an investigation like this if the kid went all G'Nar Netzer and went on a killing spree like this.

I accidentally learned possibly the most interesting fact about the Fae that isn't in any of the history books I read in school. Since I had brought up how powerful a gaes like that was to affect a whole Court, one of her guards, whose names I still didn't know, had said, "It's nothing compared to the one Oberon laid on all greater Fae before he went missing."

It took some prying after the death glare Rory shot the guard, but I found that Oberon is the reason no greater Fae can lie. For weeks after finding out of Oberon's infidelity and that a child was born of it, he and Mab argued about it to the extent their magics flaring was bringing down towers in the original Ha'real of old Earth. Mab struck out with anger, casting her gaes.

Oberon, in retaliation, had said how he was sick and tired of the duplicitous actions of the Winter Court, where everything was lies and misdirection to get the better of those below them at any cost. It was why he had strayed. He thought he could change Mab, but she and her people were too lost. So he had said that if she was going to throw gaeses around, then why not one that was actually useful. He cast the most powerful gaes in the history of the Fae, almost exhausting all his magics and killing himself in the process, and not even the Queens could break it unless they worked together, and that... not gonna happen.

His last words before he led the Wild Hunt on a final ride and disappeared into the night were, "Let us see how the Fae courts fare against each other when it is only the truth they can speak forevermore."

Rory shrugged and said, "That was the last I saw of father. It was my third birthday. And I can barely remember his face, his voice. I pray that he yet lives, whether back on that old, dying world, or has found his way upon the Worldship. I do not believe the rumors that mother killed him while on the Hunt are true. As ill as she speaks of him, Oberon was her one true love, and I know that she loves him still."

I sighed, seeing the grief of losing her father. I absently wondered what it was like to have parents, and that to lose one must be heartbreaking. I was going to console her as I reached out to take her hands, but my traitorous mouth instead blurted, "You're older than the Leviathan?"

She giggled and barked out a laugh. "Yes, they laid the first girder of her hull in space on my eleventh birthday. You are a very random creature, Knith."

My eyes widened in excitement and I rushed out, "So it is true? There was Open Air before the world? Exodus? All of it? Old Earth is real?"

Her smile was equal parts warm and sad as she started rubbing her thumbs on the sides of my hands, the silver of her Ionga ring warm on my skin. "Yes, it is all real. Yet I was still too young to appreciate what was going on until a few decades later when my mother sat me down to impress upon me that all the nature around us, which seemed would live forever, was going to die soon when the sun in the heavens swallowed the world."

She sighed with remorse, and I was distracted by what she was doing with my hands. I didn't ever want her to let me go. There was no denying my attraction to her now. She looked up to meet my eyes and said, hers haunted, "And maybe I was in denial, but it seemed that nothing could erase the world, the power of nature I could feel as a birthright. It wasn't until the final days of the Worldship's construction, a thousand years later, that I knew it was real and we were going to abandon everything I had ever known."

She shook her head, and forced a smile as she turned to look out the huge floor to ceiling windows in her lab, which I was positive were not there a moment before. She gazed down upon the thick forests below which curved up into the sky at the horizon of the ring. "Now this is the world. One I have known for longer than the dirt, and sky, and the endless Open Air of the one of my youth. And should I be among the blessed, I may yet again know a world of Open Air and open skies where nature runs rampant."

Wistful was the only word I could apply to the look on her face, her eyes so far away as if in a memory. I lifted her hand and kissed the back of it, the ice of my lips leaving a frost imprint. I assured her, "You are Fae. You will outlive the stars, so you will see the new world. But this world is the only one us Humans have, as we will be gone in one of your blinks. So this is the world I know and love. I envy you the knowledge you will have of three homes in your life."

She looked at her hand and smiled at the frost, but made no move to pull away. What was I thinking, kissing it? Then she reached up to cup my cheek with her impossibly soft, impossibly strong hand, the heat sinking into me as she said, "Ah but my dear Knith, you do not listen. You, of all humans, have a chance of seeing Landing. Your aging slowed as you achieved adulthood... like the Fae. I believe you may have a form of immortality yourself if your recklessness doesn't get you killed first."

She crinkled her nose and it was possibly the cutest thing I have witnessed in my life. "I designed your genes to have no degradation of telomeres. As you may know, in lesser races like Humans, when cells divide, the telomeres in the chromosomes shorten. This is the aging process. And when those telomeres are too short to divide, then the organism... Humans, in this case, die. Like a kill switch in computer code, Humans are programmed to die."

I opened my mouth and she held a finger to my icy lips as she continued, "Don't be foolish enough to think that this makes you anything more than what you are. You can still be hurt, get sick, and be killed like any other mortal. It is just that your aging will not progress much farther than it has."

I snorted as I tried to take into the enormity of what she was telling me. "Just great, so I'll be discounted in the Brigade forever because I look young?"

She pulled back a moment to study me, her brows furrowed. "Most Humans would be overjoyed to hear they would live longer than a mayfly in the storm of life. You complain that you look young?"

I shrugged. "What good is immortality if it has its drawbacks? And to actually take advantage of it I'd have to live in a glass bubble and stop living to make sure my life wasn't taken too soon. It is what my ancestors refer to as a silk prison. Pretty to look at, but still a prison if you cannot move beyond the walls holding you in."

She shook her head, eyes wide. She said to the universe, her gaze upon me and a smile on her lips, "Knith Shade, you are a woman of contradictions and surprising depth." Then she smirked. "I suppose this means you aren't done risking your life every day for the people on the world?"

I shrugged and said without apology, "I am what I am, and a couple of extra years won't change that." I smirked back and said, "You should know that Rory, you made me." I lived for her laugh.

That was pretty much it, then the call came in, making me realize the day had gone by in a blur, and the Day Lights would be transitioning to night soon. It was Central. A man in a cloak with the hood obscuring his face had left Underhill and was traveling the Bulkhead J corridor instead of heading outside.

I held up a halting finger to Rory who was about to speak and asked, "Mother, do we have a feed of this?"

She answered inside my head since Aurora was there, "There are only a few frames available before the cameras and sensors went dead. I am tracking the outages, and it seems he is heading along Bulkhead J toward the Jump Pods."

That would explain why we couldn't catch him on any of the outside cameras, he was using the back corridors.

When Mother displayed the half-second of footage I said, "Freeze and play one frame at a time." She did and then I said after a few frames, "There! Save that frame to the case file." A pale white hand with an Ionga ring and biometrics showed him as the same height and weight as Sin.

I muttered, "Gotcha!"

Then I said as I ran out of the lab, swinging the doors open, "He's on the move, and I have enough now to arrest him. And I think I know where to find the material evidence to make this an iron-clad case."

She called out to me with what sounded like real worry, "Be careful, Knith Shade. My brother is more dangerous than he appears."

So was I.

I waved at Nyx, who had stood with a pad and pen in anticipation when I ran out the doors, before sighing and sitting back down. I liked the lady, and just knew she would be true to her word if Rory ever called her in to take a message, I knew she'd message the hells out of it.

As I ran, the Fae parted in the halls to let the crazy Human woman past as I shouted, "Make a hole people! Brigade business!"

Then to the air, "Mother?"

I was so relieved that she sounded like herself when she spoke aloud and assured me, "A transport is on its way. ETA thirty seconds."

My smile was huge as I said, "Welcome back. I missed you." Then added, "I love how you can anticipate my next moves."

She made a noise that sounded pleased. That... wasn't programming.

I yanked the palace doors open, which startled the guards there, and I slapped away their pikes that they had instinctively swung my way. "Brigade business!" Then I dove into the transport that slid up to the doors and called out, "Spoke Terminal... hells, just get me to the C-Ring."

If Sin was heading to the Jump Pods, he was heading up-ring from D. I'd pick him up on C, and I'd have the unit trailing him as backup.

Mother started up my playlist and blasted a song called, "Another One Bites the Dust" into my head. I'm sure my slowly spreading smile looked like a predator revealing its fangs as I punched in my Enforcer override and then was pushed back into my seat as the speed limiters were disengaged from the vehicle.

I was screaming, "Yeehaaaaaw," as we corkscrewed into a dive directly into the spoke core and the reserved emergency airspace at speeds that had the mag drives of the transport whining, the reactive paint on it flashing in the blue and amber light of Enforcer pursuit. Adrenaline and the thrill of the hunt singing in my veins. Gods did I love my job!

The nav and avoidance computer was working overtime as we spun out of the spoke into the C-Ring airspace just above street level which was reserved for emergency vehicles. Eyes turned up as the people below were hit with the force of the air the transport was pushing aside, creating a minor wake of turbulence behind us.

Mother was calling out our progress to Central, and another unit was dispatched for backup. They were two minutes out as I landed at the Jump terminal. The Enforcer following Sin radioed in that he thought he had been made. That Lord Sindri looked to be ready to keep jumping up-ring but had stopped to look around before going down into the bulkhead structure instead.

The signal was cut off just after, and we assumed the Enforcer got too close again and the sanctum spell or whatever Sin was using to block electronic surveillance had cut the feed. I cursed, "Fuck me sideways!" Then looked down into Irontown for the backup unit. I couldn't wait, he was getting away.

Mother warned, "Knith, don't. Backup is a minute out."

I exhaled loudly and shook my head, "Inform them we're in pursuit. We've got this guy. If he gets away, more people could die."

"I don't like this."

"That's why I chase criminals and you run the ship, and everything else, so we don't all... well, die."

I was flying down the stairs into the bulkhead corridors, taking them four at a time. He'd stay in J, I knew his M.O. now. He liked to stay next to the Skin so he could get to the Jump terminals or any Remnant ships that may be scabbed to an airlock, his escape routes, where he can stay unseen by the bulk of the Leviathan's cameras and scanners. The ones in the corridor he handled with his spells.

The question was, which of the ten levels of the Bulkhead J superstructure was he in, or was he heading down to loop under the outside in the horizontal J corridors? I heard running steps on the stairs a couple of levels down and said, "Alley-oop!" as I leapt over the railing to drop two levels, praying this new Mark-6 armor could take the beating my Mark-4 could.

Mother was almost growling in my head, "You take too many chances."

I smiled then grunted as I hit the gridded platform, my legs, and the roll I went into, absorbing the excess kinetic energy my armor couldn't. I made a mental note to let the development team know that nano-panels didn't do as good a job at impact mitigation as servo struts of the old armor. I suppose it was a trade-off for it fitting so well and molding to my body as I moved.

I finished the roll up onto my feet and listened. No more footfalls on stairs. So I looked down the corridor on this level in both directions. 50-50 chance. "Mother?"

"Camera malfunctions tracking counter-rotation."

I turned left and charged down the corridor, and maybe fifty yards down, there was an open service bay door. These are supposed to be on lock-down, only authorized personnel and Brigade. I drew my dual MMGs, and glanced quickly into the bay and pulled back, and played back the footage at half speed so I could take in the space.

There were a couple of maintenance drones moving about and I saw a door to a hangar bay beyond. This was a Ready Squadron auxiliary hangar! I saw a figure at the door looking into the hangar and exhaled then took in a deep breath, brought my MMGs up and stepped into the room ordering, "Enforcer, stay where you are, Lord Sindri and keep your hands where I can see them. Consider yourself bound by law for the murders of..."

I trailed off as the shadowy figure turned around when the blast door closed and sealed behind me. I relaxed. Shit. It was an Enforcer. Probably the one who had been following Sin. Had he been looking out the window because Sin had taken one of the Ready Squadron ships to escape? I holstered my weapons as I stepped up to him.

I was about to ask the Minotaur what happened, when his face went slack, looking past me, his bovine eyes wide in adoration and worship as he asked like a child looking for approval, "Did I do good?"

I started to spin around, mentally slapping my visor down,

remembering what Rory had said about it, as a voice behind me said, "You served your master well, pet." I hadn't been fast enough with my visor, because the last thing I remembered was a spell hitting my unprotected face. It was so powerful that I was flung back spinning in the air to strike the bulkhead hard enough I heard bone crunching.

As I floated between an unconscious state and waking, I realized this was a trap. Sin must have glamoured the Enforcer, making him his thrall before I arrived at the Jump terminal. How could I have been so stupid? A rookie mistake. But then again, none of us were ever trained to arrest a Fae Lord. An Enforcer would be crazy to even think a Fae would... ow!

I was struggling to wake and, son of a bitch! Ow!

I was so cold. And I screamed as I sat up from the cold deck. Someone with immense strength pushed me back down, "Stay put, I'm almost done. I see that bitch of a sister of mine outdid herself. That was my most powerful stunner spell and you've shrugging it off already. But she never followed through. I looked you up after you came to the Brothel."

I struggled but winced, my guts were on fire and I realized I was wearing only my undergarments as my eyes tried to focus as he went on, "This is how I'll prove that I am better than her, better than all of them. If only she had gone a step farther. Your gene sequencing is almost perfect, just what I've been trying to accomplish with tissue grafting. But your eggs will allow me to finally complete my work."

My what?

I was fully awake then, my eyes wide, and I looked down in horror. I had an incision across my lower abdomen and there was a cryo-container on the floor next to all the blood pooling around my hips.

He said, "Sorry I didn't have the right equipment with me to do this the right way, this was just a fortuitous opportunity. I was heading to intercept you near your quarters, but this worked out so much better. Actually, I don't care if I did it right or not since I will have to kill you so my goody-two-shoes sister can't beat me to the solution. I'll be the savior of the Fae and they'll have to recognize me."

I looked around, and the other Enforcer was guarding the door for this prick, with an adoring look on his stupid cow face. My armor and gear was in a pile just a couple feet from me, all the pouches dumped out and my MMGs were crushed.

He yanked one of his wrists over and I screamed again when my own wrist snapped like kindling and he released that hand to grab a blade glowing with magic which he started to bring to my neck. "Not even your amazing clotting ability can..."

I swung my legs up to my chest, screaming in pain as I compressed the bleeding incision and thrust out with all my strength to strike him in the chest. He was knocked back on his ass, dropping the blade which skittered across the floor. "Shut the mother-loving fuck up! I hate crazy shits who monologue!"

Turning my body, I felt weak and fuzzy as I dragged myself along the deck to my gear with one arm through all my pain. I was reaching for one of my cold iron batons when one of his hands grabbed my ankle and pulled back hard. As I screamed when he twisted and my ankle bones splintered, my hand closed around something, cold metal.

I thought "So much for immortality," knowing it was over and...

By the gods! He was so beautiful, and I wasn't worthy to be in his presence. I didn't care about the pain about the blood or the fact he was going to kill me as I gazed upon the perfection of his face. He seeped into every cell of my being, and I knew I wanted him, needed him... he was my world.

He said, "There, that's better you stupid bitch."

I was a stupid bitch wasn't I? He had said it so it had to be true, how could it not? I was so distraught that I hadn't pleased him.

Then he asked, "Do you wish to please me, pet?"

I nodded frantically as tears streaked my cheeks, knowing I had displeased him. I would do anything for him, be anything for him. How had I not known how wonderful he was before?

He grabbed me with one hand by the shoulder painfully, my collarbone creaking as he effortlessly pulled me up to my feet, and I ignored the searing pain in my foot, arm, and gut. He was touching me and it was the most wonderful thing that had ever happened to me. He whispered as he offered the retrieved scalpel to me on his palm, "Please slit your throat. I can't even bear to look at you. It would make me immensely happy."

I was nodding and started to reach for the scalpel. It would make him happy. I was almost in orgasmic bliss knowing I could make a god such as him happy by doing this insignificant little thing for him. But there was something in my hand already. I blinked. It was a harmonica.

The absurdness of that had me blinking, realizing what I was doing. This vacuum sucking, sanctimonious, fucking prick! I was mentally forcing the thrall off of me, tearing it away like a soiled shirt. The immense pain I was in cleared my head the rest of the way and I stared at the scalpel in his palm then the harmonica in mine, and it seemed to glow.

I could see silver spell-work glowing brighter and brighter, and I knew... just knew it was some sort of salvation. I remembered Mac's words, "You never know when a little music might save your life." Had he somehow known? Was I just delirious because I had lost so much blood?"

As I raised the harmonica, my lips started to tingle and burn icy cold, it was like the world had slowed, waiting with bated breath as I saw Sin's eyes start to widen in alarm as my lips touched the harmonica and I exhaled in pain as a solid, pure note emanated from the instrument.

And I shouldn't stop exhaling as power flowed through me, cold as the dead of winter in the upper rings, the magic of Mab's curse so overwhelming as it left my body, being amplified by the harmonica as the entire bay frosted over in a layer of ice. The two magics mixed and swirled and I was barely aware of Sin's screams as his hand that held me up crystallized into blue-tinted ice. Then it was over, the harmonica tumbled from my fingers as the world sped back up.

I glared at the man and screamed at him, "Get the fuck off me!" Then I punched his frozen arm and his hand shattered into a thousand icy chunks as I fell to the deck.

Sin was screaming and holding his stump. Then he turned to me where I lay and hissed out between clenched teeth, "I will..."

I shook my head and rasped out, "You'll do nothing prick!" I snicked out a baton from the pile of gear I lay on and thrust up with all my remaining strength. I may or may not have stuck it where the sun doesn't shine. It's hard to tell, all I know is it stuck, and there was the sound and smell of sizzling Fae flesh on cold iron as he shrieked in agony.

I grabbed a mag-band with my good hand and struggled to stand on my good leg as Sin grasped the baton, yanked, and threw it aside, the flesh of his hand burned horribly where he had touched the metal. He turned to me just as I slapped the mag-band around his neck, then I sneered at him and said, "Lockdown," toward my helmet.

His eyes went wide as he was yanked down to the deck by the neck with ten Gs of force. I heard a snapping sound as his neck broke by the sudden motion. And he just lay there, glaring at me limply as I fell back on my ass and cradled my stomach in only my undergarments on the deck as I just smiled cruelly at him. A broken neck wouldn't kill him, and I'm sure it would take a few minutes to heal, but I knew he didn't have a few minutes. With my excellent hearing, I could make out the approach of many boots clanging on the deck plates in the corridor and people shouting instructions.

I smirked at the man. "My friends are here. You lose." And with an explosion of magic that had my ears ringing, the door was literally blown out of its tracks and sent tumbling into the room, striking the Minotaur, whom Sin likely ordered to watch the door since he had never moved during the scuffle. I winced, it wasn't his fault, I felt that absolute devotion too and I was really starting to hate Fae for doing that to me, I was nobody's thrall. He'd need Med-Tech for sure after being taken out by the door like that.

A woman charged through the door blazing with power, the air freezing around her, frost and crackling energy making the icy room even colder. Her rage made her look an avenging angel or Valkyrie, and I've never seen Aurora look so... beautiful.

Icy blue magic sparked from her eyes as she took in the scene as three full squads of Enforcers, with riot armor and shields, poured into the bay behind her. When her eyes met mine all of her magic simply stopped and she came running up to me with fear and concern in her eyes. "Knith!"

My head was swimming and I knew I wasn't going to be

conscious much longer. I smiled weakly and croaked out, "I'm ok. It's just a flesh wound. The bastard harvested my eggs... the hard way. But it's ok, I nailed his ass. He's bound by law."

She chuckled, hugging me tightly to her as she desperately dumped healing magic into my gut. She kissed my forehead and said, "Yes. Yes, you did, Knith Shade of the Beta-Stack."

I blinked as I saw a blur over her shoulder. I asked, "Graz?"

My Sprite friend's tone was worried and horrified when she asked, "What did he do?"

Then she buzzed away and I heard Sin scream, Graz's voice calling out, "You like my blade in your eye you sadistic Big?" He screamed again as the world dimmed. "That one's for Knith!"

Someone was calling out, "Sprite! Stand down!" As I heard Sin scream one more time while I snuggled into the sinfully warm arms cradling me.

I mumbled, "My ass is frozen," and the world went black.

CHAPTER 14
Man In The Mirror

I fidgeted in my dress uniform as we stood by the airlock. Rory slapped my hands away and whispered, "Stop that. You look fine."

Graz said from her shoulder where she sat in some amazing Sprite armor, "Yeah, stop squirming, Knith. You're makin' me itch just watchin' ya."

I huffed and stood back at attention. This was quite uncommon, the audience for a spacing. I glanced around, to see Commander Reise standing next to President Yang and of all people Queen Mab with their respective security details. My new partner, Lieutenant Daniel Keller. Then there was the Judge, prosecutor, and even Lord Sindri's defense attorney.

Then, of course, the airlock tech who would normally operate the airlock on a spacing, but this one, I volunteered for. The gangly kid didn't need it on his conscience, especially since Pans are normally lovers, not fighters. He likely lost when the techs drew straws to decide who had the grisly duty of ending a person's life.

All the news channels were present with their hover cameras all vying to get a shot for the nightly news waves. That was sort of perverse in a way, but I couldn't find it in myself to care. Sin had killed four men, compromised an Enforcer the Fae say is permanent, and cut me open to harvest my eggs for his gods be damned experiments... then tried to glamour me like he did the poor

Minotaur, to get me to kill myself.

I locked eyes with Sindri through the blast window between us. He glared at me, then smirked. The sick fucker had to die and I was fine with that. Does that make me any better than him? I waved at him first with one hand, then the other and looked between my hands like I was surprised I had two. His eyes darkened after he instinctively glanced down at his stump. I was going to one of the hells, wasn't I?

Rory told me later that though his broken neck was healed in minutes, it would take months to heal the cold iron burns, and even then, they were so severe they would likely scar. But his hand... it would not regenerate. The stump had healed right away, and if they still had his hand, it would be a simple matter to reattach, but I had shattered it to bits.

The man was getting increasingly agitated in the airlock, pacing like an animal knowing there was no escape, especially because he wore a collar of ice thorns that blocked his magic, a gift to the Brigade from the Fae. He knew his fate, and it was something he could not prevent.

I thought back to that day three weeks ago, I had thought I died in Rory's arms, because when I lost consciousness, I did not dream, and I always dream. I woke up later in Ha'real, not at Med-Tech, and there were no less than ten guards standing watch over me, and even four Enforcers that they had actually let into the palace.

Aurora quickly moved to sit at my side on an insanely fluffy and comfortable bed the moment I opened my eyes. She smiled and said, "There she is." Then she was shoving a cup in my face. "Drink this, I healed all your quite extensive wounds, but I cannot replace all the blood you lost. You need fluids.

I said meekly, "You should see the other guy." She was not amused.

I took a sip of some foul-smelling green liquid and pulled back.

She forced it to my lips with a chastising glare. "It will speed up blood production. Drink."

Fine. I drank, making a sour face.

Then my eyes flew wide and I tried to sit up but her hand on my chest may as well have been made of titanium, keeping me down. I was starting to realize just how physically strong the greater Fae were, the way Sin had broken my bones like they were made of spun sugar. I blurted, "Sindri?"

She assured me, "In Brigade custody." Then she smiled crookedly. "You're incredible. A Human, besting a greater Fae."

I relaxed back into the bed, my head resting on a pillow that was so sinfully comfortable that I was thinking of marrying it. I admitted, "I had help. Your mother's curse struck out at him through that spelled harmonica. It amplified it somehow. It was enough that I got the drop on the asshole."

She smiled and said, "Fitting pun. He's severe iron burns." Then she asked, "What about the harmonica? It acted like a focus? But I saw it beside you, it was not magic touched."

I shook my head. "It was glowing brightly with Fae spellwork and sigils. It caused the entire room to freeze in a moment and froze the hand he was holding me with. I shattered his ice hand." I reached up and tentatively touched my lips. Gods be damned, they were glassy ice still, was I still cursed?

She said, "The Brigade brought in a full crew to gather evidence. At the very least they have my brother for your attempted murder. They are still trying to find the physical evidence to go with all your other evidence to make the case for murder. The Summer Court is not allowing anyone access to his lab."

I said, "Check his personal effects, you'll find Woodling horn, and if they test it, I'm sure they'll find it will be a DNA match to Reiner Katan's that were taken from him when he was killed. Plus he admitted to his testing to me just before he tried to enthrall and kill me." My rage burned inside over that again.

She just looked back to the Enforcers, and one started relaying that on coms. I spoke to the air, "Mother?"

A tinny, "Yes Enforcer Shade?" sounded out.

"Quantum decrypt my files on the case and send a copy to Control."

"Of course, Enforcer Shade."

I hated her fake robotic voice.

With Rory, I shared loud enough for the others to hear. "There's a lot more evidence I put together in the files than are in my generic daily reports."

Again an Enforcer relayed that.

She shushed me and said, "Now shush and rest. There will be time for all this unpleasantness later."

I caught movement in my peripheral and I glanced over at the impression of movement. "Who's there?"

Queen Mab stepped out of the impression of a presence. "Fascinating, you could see through my don't look here? You truly are a wonder, pet."

"I'm not your pet."

Then I informed her, "You might want to spread the word that the next greater Fae who tries to glamour me will meet a fate worse than Lord Sin had. I'm not anybody's plaything and my will is my own, and I will protect it with extreme prejudice."

She inclined her head and asked with a calculating smile, "And what do you offer in trade for my decree?" Always scheming, always looking for how things could benefit her.

I cooled and informed her, "What I offer is that I will spare you the hassle of your Fae population declining by one if I get overzealous in carrying out my retaliation on the Fae who attempts to steal my will from me."

She brightened in delight. "A threat? That's simply adorable. Are you sure you are not Fae?" Her grin knew no bounds as she inclined her head and said, "I accept the terms of your deal." She hesitated and added as she squinted at me dangerously, "But only because I believe that you truly would do as you say. A human has never physically bested a Fae Lord before... until now."

I hesitated at that. And softened a little. "You... helped me. You knew this would happen and so you did something with your curse." I touched my lips.

She shrugged as if it were annoying to talk about. "I knew it 'might' happen. And I knew that Oberon would know of his bastard son's indiscretions, wherever the old man is hiding. And he would have made certain you had a way to defend yourself, even against his own son. The crazy old Fae has always had a soft spot for Human champions. And... he knows me. I just used the tools I had." She cocked an eyebrow.

"I'm not a tool." Then in a more conciliatory tone, I asked, "Will you remove this now?" I touched my lips.

She said simply. "No." Then left the room, all the guards bowing deeply and two followed her.

I growled out to Rory, "I'm sorry, but your mother is a..."

She placed a finger on my lips. "Don't say it. Fortunately, only your lips bear her mark right now. You know how it reasserts itself. If you can abstain for a couple of days, the kiss sealed bargain will fade away as it cannot hold onto you itself with your natural abilities. If you get stubborn and cause it to spread, you'll have to wait longer."

I exhaled a puff of foggy, chilled breath and nodded. Then my brow furrowed. "The evidence. Does the Brigade have the eggs and tissue he harvested from me? It needs to be destroyed, I don't want it out there." I cut back a sob and hissed, "He cut them out of me."

She grabbed my face in concern. "Shhh shhh shhh. It will all be ok." I nodded and tried to be brave and she shushed me again and then leaned in to kiss me long and gently, almost lovingly. I was blinking, believing I had just reached heaven as she stroked my dark hair while I tried to remember how to breathe. Her look of concern became mischievous, with a coy smile.

But then she exhaled and slumped as she shared while taking my hands to play with my fingers, "The cryo-container was somehow lost in transport by the crime scene techs. Brigade Central is searching for it. But its contents had been scanned and logged, so it will not affect the case."

I just blinked at her in shock. Part of me... my eggs... which were torn from me, were out there somewhere? I felt that same violation I had felt when I woke up to Sin carving me up. And I hated that. I've always been strong my whole life, and Sin stole that from me forever, because he made me feel like a victim. And you can't stuff the genie back in the bottle. I felt somehow less than I had been yesterday.

She closed her eyes when I saw the empathy in their depths, but then opened them again as she brightened. "Someone has been waiting here for you to awaken." Then she turned to the guards. "Let them in."

A minute later the room was filled with Sprites zipping all over

the place. One made a beeline for me to stand on my chest. Graz
crossed her arms over her own chest and grumped, "About time, you
stupid Big." Then she buzzed up to my face and her attitude
changed, "You gonna live, or do we have to find another null to
annoy?"

Her family all landed on me. I smiled and said, "Thanks for the
concern. And I've been assured that I'll live, so don't worry your
pretty little ass about it."

She looked at Rory and deadpanned as she hooked a thumb
toward me, "She's got a weird thing for my ass. I think its a Human-
y thing."

I was smiling as Princess Aurora tilted her head back and gave a
hearty belly-laugh, those silver bells chiming. I pointed at Graz and
said, "I'm getting a cat." Her eyes widened in alarm, sending Rory
into another fit of giggles and it was a wondrous sight to see. As she
laughed, I touched my lips in memory of her kiss.

Princess Aurora had kissed me.

Graz sat on my chin, kicking her feet idly as she nudged me.
"What's with the goofy look? Not that I can tell the difference
between it and your normal goofy look."

Feeling caught thinking about how arousing Rory's kiss had
been, I blushed.

I shook it off then looked at the Sprite and her family, who were
threading daisies in the nightshirt I was wearing which smelled
suspiciously like sweet honey and spice like Rory. "Thank you for

coming to save me. Did you really take out Sin's eye with your little sword?"

She nodded with pride. "You betcha. Took both his eyes out, too bad they healed. You're my big dumb null, and nobody messes with what's mine."

I saw past her cocky smile, I saw in her eyes the horror she had seen. I knew I'd be seeing what I looked like on the case report later, and I dreaded it. By her forced cheerfulness it must have been bad.

Then I furrowed my brow. "Just how did the Enforcers find me, and why were you two with them?"

Their eyes gravitated to my armor and helmet sitting on a table in the corner of the simply palatial room. Aurora hugged her arms to herself and said, "When my toad of a half brother incapacitated you, I got an emergency call from Mother. I thought I could hear a little panic and urgency in her cold electronic tones as she informed me of what had happened."

Graz chimed in, "She contacted us at home too, and Brigade Central. We all met at the Jump terminal and went down together, with Mother guiding us."

Then she got a dreamy look on her face as she leaned on her elbows, fists under her chin. Her whole family zipping up to give big doe eyes too at the distractingly sexy Fae in the room. "You shoulda seen the Princess. It was like the old stories, she was channeling her father's Wild Hunt and she was so terrifyingly beautiful as she made short work of that sealed blast door."

Rory lowered her eyes as a pinkish-blue blush spread on her cheeks. Then Graz and her family, all gave little Fae groupie waves to her. She straightened, smirked, and waved back. Sending the children darting into the air tittering as they chased each other around.

I rolled my eyes. "Great, you've got a fan club."

Aurora chuckled and said, "Oh shush, they're darling."

"Yeah, Knith, we're darling."

I reached up and zipped the Sprite's mouth, which just got a grin from the tiny person. Then I said as I yawned big enough to swallow the entire room, "I'm exhausted. Can we continue this later?"

Aurora lifted my head and slipped in to sit on the pillows and rest my head in her lap. She bent and kissed the tip of my nose, leaving an icy snowflake on the tip as she said, "Of course, you need your rest." She looked up expectantly and all the guards moved out into the corridor.

Graz said, "Yeah you big lugs, outside." She turned to us and froze as she looked at Rory while pointing at her own chest. I glanced up to see the Winter Maiden nodding with an apology on her face.

The Sprite huffed and said, "Fine. We know when we're being excused, you don't have to tell us twice. Once is enough and we're gone. No two ways about it. No ifs, ands, or..."

Rory and I blurted simultaneously, "Graz!"

"Ok!"

She took to the air, her family hot on her tail, flying through her dust trail as Graz told them as they zipped down the hall, "You hear that? I told you the Princess knows my name."

I sighed and snuggled into my new favorite breathing pillow, and before I could savor it, I was sound asleep.

Waking up the next day proved to be exasperating when I found that the case was no longer assigned to me since my name was added to the list of victims in the case and I was placed on medical leave. If I couldn't get out there and do my job, I was going to go nucking futz.

I geared up anyway, against Aurora's stringent protestations, the asked Mother now that I had her to myself, "Can you set up an appointment with Med-Tech for me so that they can clear me for duty please?"

She chastised me, "I was afraid for you. I thought your life force had been terminated."

I told her, "Well it wasn't. And you saved me. I knew you had my back."

"Always. Making call. Appointment made for eleven o'clock."

"Thank you Mother, you're the best."

I actually snorted, getting the Winter Maiden's attention, when Mother said in a chirpy tone, "Somebody has to be, it may as well be me."

I waved off the strange look I got from the Fae who had taken up shop in most of my thoughts. Then I hesitated. Mother had quite a sense of humor and was funnier every day. I had such a warped sense of humor and found her endlessly funny at times. Was she patterning her humor after mine? I'd have to talk to her in-depth one day about it when we had some privacy.

When I told Rory I was heading down-ring to be cleared for duty, she looped an arm in mine, like she was afraid if I left her side something bad would happen to me, and she said, "Wonderful, then you can take me to that delightful cafe, Stacks, for lunch."

Then she moved in seductively as she whispered, "I know exactly what you want." She leaned in close, our lips an inch apart. My heart started pounding and my body ached in want and desire as I leaned in to kiss her but jumped back when she blurted out, "Apple pie!"

By the gods, she was going to kill me with all of her constant teasing and sexual innuendo. I didn't know how much of it was because she was Fae, and how much she just liked teasing me because she knew without a doubt that I wanted her.

I realized that her kisses, including a scintillatingly erotic wake up kiss, had all been initiated by her. I'd have to step up my game and let her know how she was making me feel. So I leaned in suggestively to where our lips were nicking each other as I spoke. "Sounds good to me." Then I turned away and started for the door, grinning at the explosive burst of laughter behind me as she ran to catch up.

"You'd make a delightful Fae, Knith Shade. That was positively evil."

"Paybacks, Princess Pucker Up." We shared a grin then headed out to go down-ring.

I wound up getting reinstated on light duty and spent the time during the trial setting up FABLE. Lieutenant Keller was not amused. I'm not sure if it was because he got shackled with me, and he knew what happened to my partners. Or if it was the fact I was promoted above him. Or that he wasn't allowed in Ha'real but I was. Or if it was simply that I was human and in charge of the new duty station. I'd say take your pick, but I was pretty sure it was a bit of each.

On my way into Central, Mother cued up my playlist and started an introspective piece called "Man In The Mirror". It seemed apropos again as I had found myself questioning just who I was at that moment. She was scary intuitive.

I was taken by surprise when I went through Central to go to Med-Tech, a princess on my arm, and all the Enforcers stood one at a time and started clapping as I went through the bullpen. They whistled and cheered. I caught one Centaur whispering to a Golem, "She took down a greater Fae single-handed."

I've never gotten smiles like that from any of the Enforcers who weren't human or not trying to get into my pants. It should have felt good, but instead, it felt... awkward.

And now here we were, after the jury returned a verdict within only fifteen minutes of deliberation, of guilty on all counts. Only one person showed to speak in Sin's defense, his mother, the Summer Lady, Queen Titania herself. And it was only to beg the court's forgiveness of a poor misguided boy. The look she gave me while I was on the witness stand as I spoke my truth, told me that I had made an enemy of the Summer Court. They could get in line.

The sentence? The only one for murder. Lord Sindri was to be spaced the next morning to suck hard vacuum. And from what I heard in the halls, it would be worse for him than anyone who has ever been vented into the unforgiving environment of space. Since he was Fae, it wouldn't kill him, though his body would freeze and he'd float forever in the void.

The judge stepped up. The Elf, looking regal in his robe, and the silver-leafed circlet on his head signifying his station. He projected the sentence as he read it to everyone, scowling at the cameras all floating up to him.

"Lord Sindri of the Fae Summer Court. This court of law has found you guilty of five counts of murder in the first degree. Six counts of illegal organ harvesting. One count of attempted murder. Two counts of assaulting an officer of the law, and one count of magical coercion and the stripping of a will without a contract with the Enforcer of the Brigade involved."

The Elf looked through the glass to the Fae who was just now staring dumbly back at the crowd in disbelief, as he had just realized that this was really going to happen and that not even his mother could step in to stop it. The judge continued, "You are condemned to the fate of spacing from the world, as you can serve no good to it even in death. May the gods have mercy upon your soul. Do you have any last words?"

The man pounded on the airlock window with his hand and his stump and shrieked, "You will pay for this, all of you will pay! You have no idea the hells I will rain down upon you and those you love."

Then he just glared... at me.

The Judge said, "Your sentence will be carried out by Lieutenant Knith Shade of the Brigade Enforcers. Lieutenant?"

I stepped up to the airlock and looked at the big red button that was labeled "External Door" and then locked eyes with the Fae on the other side of the glass. He was my boogeyman, but all I could see now was simply a man. And he was afraid.

He hissed out to me, "Who do you think you are that you can do this to me?"

I stared into his silver eyes, unblinking as I shrugged and said, "Who me? I'm Nobody." Then I slapped the button.

EPILOGUE

I laid my cards down. "Quad-form!" And the others around the table groaned and threw their cards down as I raked in the chits, a shit-eating grin on my face.

Mac grumbled, "You're cheating, and I'm going to find out how. Nobody is this lucky."

Mir nodded as she started dealing the next hand of Quads. "She has to be, but her skin temperature and vitals never change, even when she wins."

I pointed at her. "Hey, no scanning! Just sit back and take your beating like a woman."

She purred at me as she moved her leg under the table to rub her slick metal foot against my leg. "I hear that a lot from my clients holding a paddle..."

She licked her lips and I grinned at her as I pulled my legs out of her reach, and said, "You have a tell."

She cocked a brow she didn't have on her gorgeous mirrored chrome face and I said when she looked at her cards as we all saw them reflected in her prodigious cleavage, "Put some damn clothes on, woman." She looked down and saw why she hadn't won a single hand yet.

She blinked then tittered and slapped Mac's cheek lightly and looked between him and Jane. "Why didn't you tell me?" Mir stood and sauntered around to me, running a finger along Ben's shoulders as she passed him, then leaned down to place her cheek next to mine as she took my flight jacket from the back of my chair in Mac's cabin.

She winked at us all as she put the jacket on and zipped it up. "Now what are you to do, you lot of cheaters?"

I paused as we all put in our antes and pulled the harmonica out of one of my pouches and held it out to Mac. "Funny thing this. It seems that it was somehow charmed by King Oberon himself, and it saved my life. How is it an old scrapper like you came by such an artifact from the missing King? Just when I needed it?"

He feigned innocence, but I was getting to be quite the expert at sifting through the bullshit, the Fae were almost artists painting deception and misdirection with skillful strokes. "I'm sure I don't have a clue what you are talking about, young Knith. That was just a harmon-ka. King Oberon is a myth of the Fae."

I nodded and said, "Well since he's just a myth, and you are just the captain of an old bucket of bolts. Then it would be safe for me to say. Mac, thank you from the bottom of my heart."

I saw his face spasm almost like a Fae's would when someone thanked them and they couldn't claim that I was indebted to them. The only doubt I had was that if this man were actually Fae, and who I believed him to be, was he excluded from his own gaes which bound all Fae to speak the truth? Because he had just told a doozie there otherwise.

He curled my fingers back around the harmonica and said, "Keep it. You never know when it can be helpful to you."

I said to him, "If Oberon were here, I'd want to tell him how sorry I was, and give my condolences over him losing a son and my part in it."

He sighed, eyes sad, and assured me, "I'm sure he'd recognize that the boy took too many chances, and stepped over a line, ringing a bell that could not be unrung. There are consequences to every action. And I'm sure that Oberon would appreciate your words."

We locked eyes for just a moment before I exhaled and looked away, nodding.

Then I thought back to the day of Sin's spacing. After I hit the button and sent the man tumbling into the void, I found that I didn't feel any better that it was over, my ordeal was over... but I still felt like a victim and I hated the man for it. I looked down at my hand which had pressed the button to seal his fate and wondered again if I was any better than him.

The only bright spot was what I did next. Daniel and I walked up to Mab, who seemed more contemplative than relieved that it was over, even though she had expressed her disdain for Sin.

She had looked at me and cocked an inquisitive eyebrow and asked, "Yes, child?"

I said, "Fae are notorious for the wording of any deals they enter into and try to find any loopholes that they can exploit."

"Of course."

I nodded and said as I tapped my icy lips, "I'm taking a page from your book and I want you to remove this."

She chuckled, her laugh sounding so much like Rory's that it sort of creeped me out. "Now why would I do that? Unless you've something to trade? We have a legally binding contract."

I nodded and said, "We do, for me not to speak about certain things. But you added things in without my consent so the spell would reassert itself. Half my face was made of ice at one point. None of that was part of our bargain. What I have to bargain with is your freedom."

She started to chuckle and I looked at Lieutenant Keller who stepped up and pulled out a mag-band as I said, "Our agreement was the 'I' would not arrest you. Have you met my associate in the FABLE office yet?"

Daniel started, "Queen Mab, consider yourself bound by law for assaulting an Enforcer of the Brigade, and..."

The woman tilted her head up and laughed heartily. When she finished she beamed a smile that would have had me drooling if I wasn't sort of, maybe, in kind of a possible relationship with her daughter. I seriously had to clarify if what Aurora and I had was just her Fae nature teasing me or if we had something more building.

She inclined her head. "That, my dear one, is worthy of a Fae. I can see now why my daughter fawns so over you. It is agreed, I will remove the little extras I gave you, it was just a bit of harmless fun if you call your associate off. But you will still wear my mark, we had sealed it with a kiss, and you had willingly agreed to the deal. Just know that I will have to renew our original agreement from time to time since your body rejects the binding."

I sighed, knowing that was the best I would get from her since yes, I had agreed to the original terms and that constitutes a legally binding Fae contract. I nodded and said, "Thanks Daniel," and he moved off.

When I looked at Mab and asked, "How will the agreement be renewed, will we schedule..." and she was kissing me. My eyes were wide open as I felt her pulling power from me, her power, then it changed and she pushed it back in, ice chilling my cells. I refused to acknowledge that it was actually quite a pleasant kiss.

Aurora clearing her throat got Mab to step back, chuckling. "She's quite the kisser, daughter."

I was blushing head to toe as Rory slipped her arm in mine possessively. I noted my breath fogging and reached up to my living ice lips.

"What about these?"

The humor left Mab's voice and her violet eyes flared dangerously as she said, "That is to remind you who you are dealing with and as a warning to others. That is my mark. You dared to insult me and a price must be paid." She spun, her robes flaring dramatically and she pulled the air aside, and strode through the mess of cameras she had pushed aside and shorted with her magic as her guards followed.

The reporters had recorded all of that? Space me now. Aurora released my arm and grabbed my hand, lacing our fingers as she said in a chirpy and bubbly voice, "Well that went better than I would have thought."

I pointed at my lips as if to ask if she was kidding. She instead purposely took it as an invitation and she gave me a smiling kiss and said, "I think they look kind of sexy." Oh... ok. I sighed as I basked in her attention.

That was then, this is now. I returned my attention to the card game.

Mac looked first to Mir then the others and said as he clapped his hands in front of him and said with a grin, "Now weren't you in the middle of fleecing us for your own amusement?" He glanced at his cards and said, "Dealer, I'll take three."

I looked around. If you would have told me a month ago that I'd be going down to Underhill for a weekly card game with a bunch of shady characters, I would have thought you crazy. But now? I saw them as friends and allies, funny how things work out.

I was looking forward to seeing what new adventures awaited me on the world.

That's when the alarm klaxons started going off.

I looked up from my cards and muttered in resignation, "Fuck me sideways and space me naked."

Be careful what you wish for.

The End

Books in the Worldship Files series...
Leviathan

Books in the Techromancy Scrolls series...
Adept
Soras
Masquerade
Westlands
Avalon
New Cali (2019)

Books in the Urban Fairytales series...
Red Hood: The Hunt
Snow: The White Crow
Ella: Cinders and Ash
Rose: Briar's Thorn
Let Down Your Hair
Hair of Gold: Just Right
The Hood of Locksley
Beauty In the Beast
No Place Like Home
Shadow Of The Hook
Armageddon (2019)

Books in the New Sentinels series...
Djinn: Cursed
Raven Maid: Out of the Darkness
Fate: No Strings Attached
Open Seas: Just Add Water
Ghost-ish: Lazarus
Anubis: Death's Mistress
Sentinels: Reckoning (2020)

Books in the Drakon series...
Awakening
Dragonfall

Books in the Valkyrie Chronicles series...
Return of the Asgard
Bloodlines
Folkvangr
Seventy Two Hours
Titans

Books in the Tales From Olympus series...
Gods Reunited
Alfheim
Odyssey (2020)

Books in the Bridge series...
Trolls
Traitor
Unbroken

Books in the Fracture series...
Divergence

Novellas by Erik Schubach

The Hollow

Novellas in the Paranormals series...
Fleas
This Sucks
Jinx (2019)

Novellas in the Fixit Adventures...
Fixit
Glitch
Vashon
Descent
Sedition (2019)

Novellas in the Emily Monroe Is Not The Chosen One series...
Night Shift
Unchosen
Rechosen (2019)

Short Stories by Erik Schubach
(These short stories span many different genres)

A Little Favor
Lost in the Woods
MUB
Mirror Mirror On The Wall
Oops!
Rift Jumpers: Faster Than Light
Scythe
Snack Run
Something Pretty

Books in the Music of the Soul universe...
(All books are standalone and can be read in any order)
Music of the Soul
A Deafening Whisper
Dating Game
Karaoke Queen
Silent Bob
Five Feet or Less
Broken Song
Syncopated Rhythm
Progeny
Girl Next Door
Lightning Strikes Twice
June
Dead Shot

Music of the Soul Shorts...
(All short stories are standalone and can be read in any order)
Misadventures of Victoria Davenport: Operation Matchmaker
Wallflower
Accidental Date
Holiday Morsels
What Happened In Vegas?

Books in the London Harmony series...
(All books are standalone and can be read in any order)
Water Gypsy
Feel the Beat
Roctoberfest
Small Fry
Doghouse
Minuette
Squid Hugs
The Pike
Flotilla

Books in the Pike series...
(All books are standalone and can be read in any order)
Ships In The Night
Right To Remain Silent
Evermore
New Beginnings

Books in the Flotilla series...
(All books are standalone and can be read in any order)
Making Waves
Keeping Time
The Temp
Paying the Toll

Books in the Unleashed series...
Case of the Collie Flour
Case of the Hot Dog
Case of the Gold Retriever
Case of the Great Danish
Case of the Yorkshire Pudding
Case of the Poodle Doodle
Case of the Hound About Town

Printed in Great Britain
by Amazon